Touching Other Lives

Volume 4
Episodes 22-27

by

Margaret Gregory

Touching Other Lives

Volume 4
Episode List

Episode 22

Annie Gets in Trouble

Chapter 1

Abbie watched her father facing the older man and talking confidently. He seemed unfazed by some extremely personal questions. She supposed this was how people saw him when he was working at his business. If only she could be like that. Right now, she was a bundle of nerves, hardly game to say a word.

Before they had left the car to come up to this wood panelled, old fashioned office, her father had been explicit with his instructions. Don't volunteer information, just answer questions politely but briefly. He had also had her memorise several questions to ask. It sounded like he had this session planned out, even though the old man was the instigator of the meeting.

If she had her way, Abbie decided, she wouldn't even be there. How could she be the child of some heiress? Already, she had caught her father in some inconsistencies. He'd told her mother that this ex-girlfriend, the supposed heiress, had died. That was why he had become her guardian, but the woman was still alive. He said he had not been aware of the girl's family name, but he had that birth certificate for Gabrielle Hartley. The person they now thought her to be.

Now he was spinning a story about how he had met this woman and how it had come about that they'd had sex and she'd got pregnant. Abbie felt her insides writhe at the thought of her father doing that. The old man, she'd paid no attention to his name, the Hartley woman's trustee anyway, was smiling occasionally as if the things her father was saying brought back memories. Maybe he was telling the truth.

Her father was claiming to have paid the doctors' fees, and seen she had everything she'd needed for the child, but that the woman had upped and left before the birth. He claimed to have been upset because he had looked forward to being a father and had hoped she would agree to marry him. "I know she had told me she wanted a child for her Ma and Pa, I had assumed she'd gone back to them. It seems, in hindsight, she wanted it for herself."

The old man sat up straighter at that. Maybe that was true. He didn't seem to be so tight lipped and sceptical. Finally, the old man turned to her.

"This must seem unreal, Miss Carson."

Abbie nodded. It was unreal that her father had sex with a mad woman. He who was always so image conscious. If she really was a child of that union...ewww. It was also unreal that neither her father nor the old man had mentioned that Gabrielle Hartley had been one of twins.

"What do you like doing, Miss Carson?"

Abbie shrugged. She didn't have hobbies, or do sports or after school activities.

"She's interested in fashion design," Carson helped out.

"What other subjects do you like at school?" Tyrell tried again.

"I like maths, but that doesn't lead to any careers that I like," Abbie kept her tone polite as her father had insisted. She played safe and parroted her father's words – what he always insisted.

"Maude's brothers were both very good at maths," Tyrell told her. "And I have recently had Maude tested, and it seems she has an unsuspected affinity for numbers too."

"Really?" Abbie said, suddenly more interested. "I assumed that I had inherited that from my Dad." She paused then blurted,

"Do I look like her? I mean, not like she looks now, but when she was younger?"

Tyrell smiled, then twisted to open a drawer in his desk. He lifted out a photo album, and turned it so she could open it.

In spite of herself, Abbie was fascinated. The young Maude Hartley, was very blonde and very pretty, even with the odd set of her blue eyes. Abbie had blue eyes as well, although her dad's were brown. A passing thought made her wonder if the reason she had always had her hair bleached to blond, was so she would look like this woman.

Her eyes moved to the other people in the photographs, wondering if there were any with her father in. Unlikely, she told herself if her father reckoned he didn't know the family.

Tyrell identified the other people, Maude's parents, her brothers and friends of her brothers, servants. Maude was a late and unexpected child – so there was a big gap between her and her brothers. She deliberately lingered over each page, and as she hoped, the men began to talk.

"Maude never told us who the father of her child was, children actually. She had twins."

On cue, Jeremy Carson gave a perfect imitation of surprise. Surely he'd read the newspapers?

Abbie listened, picking up more inconsistencies, but she said nothing, appearing to be ignoring them.

"....so that is why it took us so long to find her children," Tyrell was saying. "We learnt of them after the trouble she got in. What was your understanding? It seems they found you quite easily."

"I understood that the department of Human services had Abbie in foster care. They never mentioned a sibling. I would have moved heaven and earth to find her if I had known."

"Seems you would have been too late," Tyrell said sadly. "Didn't you read about the find?"

Abbie tuned out. She had read the recent news, although not at home. Her father said that sort of article was just sensation seeking and claimed not to read such stuff. However, her attention was caught by a young man in the photos. He was even better looking than her father, and his face seemed more used to smiling – not like her father's.

Well, he was smiling today, Abbie corrected herself, but that was a ploy to put the old guy at ease. He never smiled much at home these days – if he ever did.

Carson leant over to see what Abbie was staring at. The blue eyed Maude and the brown eyed friend of her brothers.

Tyrell said, "Oh, his name is right there! I just can't recall it right now."

"Daddy, do I really look like her?"

Carson considered, "You won't be exactly like her, but your hair looks the same colour, and your face is a similar shape. The hair style makes you look different."

"You are a great deal like her, Miss Carson. Reserved, polite, well presented, and I think with a mind of your own."

Carson growled softly. Tyrell didn't seem to notice because he went on, "It was such a shock when I heard what had happened to you. I am so glad that you came through the ordeal so well."

"I don't want to talk about that," Abbie said, and she closed the album half way through.

Something occurred to her, that her father hadn't covered, but it came under the heading of "don't make it sound like you are greedy for the money they think you are entitled to."

"Do you think that happened because I might be your missing heiress?"

Tyrell sat back in his chair and considered Abbie, but he was also observing Carson. "We haven't made it public about the Hartley fortune being involved," he remarked. "However we did publish a couple of articles and they led us to you and your father. So perhaps, someone did add up the pieces. Does that worry you?"

Abbie nodded. "A bit, but I still don't know how you can be sure."

"Well, the board of trustees, of which I am a member, have suggested a DNA test. You, your father, and Maude. We can't finalise anything until a result is returned. Have you an objection to that?"

Abbie shrugged and looked at her father.

"It makes perfect sense," Jeremy Carson told her.

"Okay then. How do you do it?"

Tyrell called in an assistant, who was 'used to doing this new-fangled stuff', and who told them, "We use the best quality testing kits and send the swabs to the best certified lab."

"Mr Carson, I will just get you to sign a consent form, for you and your daughter."

Tyrell waited until Carson had his mouth open before saying, as if reminiscing, "Maude finally told me that the girls' father was Wally. Never did tell me the full name."

Carson made a gargling sound, and when he could speak, he said, "Heck! I'd forgotten that."

Abbie could almost believe her father's recollection, even though he claimed to have forgotten some details about the joke that had led him to being given that name by Maude. Except that her father had no sense of humour.

Chapter 2

"When might we get a result back from the lab, Mr Tyrell?"

"Oh, I will ask them to expedite it, so probably a week or two."

"The results," Carson stated, "They will be kept strictly confidential?"

"Of course," Tyrell assured him. "As you will have read on the release you signed, the details can only be used to confirm the relationship. They cannot be released for any other purpose."

Carson decided that the meeting had covered all essentials, and he stood up, gesturing to Abbie.

"I expect you will be in touch when the results are in?"

"Indeed," Tyrell agreed, standing up to shake Carson's hand again. "Then we can finalise details of the trust and how it is to be managed. Oh, and Maude is looking forward to meeting Abbie."

"Assuming your research is correct," Carson qualified. "I hope for her sake it is."

"Bye Mr Tyrell," Abbie said as she followed her father out.

Once out of the building, Carson called up a taxi to take them home.

"You did well, Abbie."

"Do you really think I am the girl they are looking for?"

"I believe so, though I thought Maude had died."

"Are you looking forward to meeting her again?" Abbie dared to ask, since her father seemed as pleased as could be.

"It will be strange," Carson admitted. "We are both a lot older now."

"What if I don't like her?"

"Just be polite. You won't be going to live with her, since

Victoria and I are your legal guardians.”

“Okay.”

“One thing though, Abbie. I wouldn’t go bragging if you are confirmed as a Hartley. Your thought about a reason for your abduction – though it’s a long shot, might be true.”

“I wasn’t going to. I don’t want everyone trying to sponge off me because they think I am suddenly filthy rich. They won’t like hearing that I would only be getting an allowance for now.”

“Good girl,” Carson praised, surprising Abbie.

Why couldn’t Dad be like this all the time?

“You would need to be careful about boys you meet too,” Carson warned. “Ones who might claim to like you but only want your money.”

A frisson of warning descended her spine. If her half sibs were correct, then her father had done that very thing to their mother. All of a sudden, Abbie decided that she didn’t want her dad to be ‘nice’. He was likely a big fat liar, lulling her into cooperation and obedience. Well, two could play that game! She wasn’t going to believe a thing he said from now on.

She glanced at her watch. “Daddy, I’m starving. Can we get something from Subway?”

Carson chuckled. “Yes, I think you deserve a treat.”

Abbie grinned to herself. Maybe, if she ate slowly, her father wouldn’t insist she go to school for the afternoon session. Then the grin faded. She wasn’t looking forward to facing her friends, given their reactions and comments on Facebook. Telling them that she might be about to become rich in her own right, might distract them, but not for long, and not if the money wasn’t going to be ‘now’. The downside was worse. If she wasn’t a Hartley, they would call her a liar and that was just the start.

The following day, when it was time to go to school, Abbie

was relieved to discover that her parents had already gone off to some business thing. Her father would have no patience with her nerves, but Mrs Buttrose had more sympathy, and gave her some advice.

"Just tell your friends that you would rather not talk of it yet. I'm sure they will understand."

Abbie didn't argue that point, because she wanted to play on the sympathy. "Could you drop me off a bit early? But around the back? I want some time to myself before everyone sees me."

"I'm not supposed to do that."

"Pleese? Just this once? I'll show you where to go."

"Alright, but not a word to your father, and I will watch you until you get into the grounds."

"Thanks," Abbie said sincerely.

"You had better get ready. Your lunch is on the kitchen table."

"Oh! I usually buy it."

"Your father feels it best if you don't let your friends expect you to buy for them too."

"You mentioned that, did you?" Abbie hid her annoyance.

"It is a kind of bullying and I didn't think it fair to you."

"I guess....but we took turns."

"All the same," Mrs Buttrose summed up. "I'm just going to get the car out."

Abbie went straight from the car to the back gate, then waved at Mrs Buttrose just before she went out of sight. She hid, and waited for her to drive off, and stayed in place waiting for little Miss Goody to arrive. She wanted to talk to Annie.

"Dusty! Wait up!"

Annie turned around. "Hi! How are you"

"I'm okay. I just wanted to ask you something."

"Okay."

"First off, where's Kemple?"

"He must be sick. He wasn't here yesterday either."

"Where was he when you found me in his shed?"

"I don't know."

"Do you think he was part of, you know, grabbing me?"

"No! Because he was helping to search the park for your phone, Friday morning."

"So how did you find where I was? I heard that pup of yours, yapping like anything."

"I had forgotten to ask Martin something and when his phone was flat, I walked back. Lucky started carrying on, and really, I thought it was Martin in the shed."

"Why didn't you go in?"

"Couldn't. The door wouldn't lift up."

"So you called the police? I'm sure Martin didn't like that."

"If he was hurt or something, he wouldn't have cared."

"Did they question him?"

"I don't know."

"They probably have him locked up."

"Abbie, if you are only interested in running Martin down, you can go off by yourself."

"Oh, alright! Are you going to tell everyone it was you who found me?"

"No."

"You'd be a hero."

"So what? I was just glad you were okay, and besides, I was told not to talk about it, not even to Martin."

"They must think he was involved."

"No, I think it was more likely they hoped whoever took you would come back if they didn't know you'd been found. So I suggest you don't say anything either."

"I wasn't going to say anything anyway. Hey, wait a bit. What day was I found?"

"Friday. Don't you remember?"

"I thought it was Saturday..."

"Maybe they let you sleep to get over it a bit. Be glad. You'd better not expect to be left alone here. Gail has been sounding off about you."

"Not just here. I saw what they put on Facebook and Messenger."

"Well, I don't mind if you want to hang out with Naomi, Karen and I."

"I think I will be fine."

"Good! You're better than any of your other friends."

"Oh, thanks for sending me your notes and stuff."

"No worries. Are you up to date?"

"Probably not. Dad made us come home so suddenly, that we didn't have time to check if more stuff was at the local post office."

"Let me know what notes you need," Annie offered.

Abbie smiled and started to walk off faster, intentionally leaving Annie behind. It wasn't hard. She was dawdling, probably hoping Kemple would turn up.

Naomi fidgeted. The bell to go into class had gone, but Annie hadn't returned. She exchanged looks with Karen.

"Maybe Aunt Sharon won't notice?"

"She will!" Naomi said dispiritedly. "She marks the book even if she doesn't call the names out."

"We will have to tell her if she asks," Karen admitted. "I don't know why she even bothers with Abbie."

"You know what she's like," Naomi pointed out.

Ms Sutton noticed that Abbie wasn't in the room and went over to Gail, Helen and Claire. She kept her voice low, but Gail, acting innocent, spoke loud enough for those nearby to hear. "I don't know where she is, Ms Sutton. She said she wanted to be alone. We thought she would come at the bell."

"Why didn't you say something?"

"We didn't want her in trouble."

Karen whispered, "Oh yeah? They are the ones who upset Abbie in the first place. From what they were saying, they do want her in trouble. Damn. We'll have to say something."

Their teacher was moving towards them now.

"Do you know where Annie is? Or Abbie?"

Karen was caught by her questioning look. "Annie went off after Abbie," she said in a very low voice. "Abbie was upset."

"I see. I will get you to take a message to Miss Castle. She can organise someone to go look for them. I assume Annie wouldn't leave the school grounds?"

"No!" Naomi confirmed immediately.

"Okay. Karen, go and tell Miss Castle what you told me. I was asked to keep an eye on Abbie. They thought there might be some after reaction to what she went through."

As Karen stood up to leave the room, Naomi noticed Gail and her two cronies quietly sniggering. When she returned, she wasn't happy.

"Miss Castle wasn't there," she told her friend. "Gill insisted on hearing the message."

"But he'll look for them?"

"Yeah, but I reckon they'll be in worse trouble. I didn't tell him where I thought they might be. I suggested the girls' toilets. I doubt that will stop him from storming in."

They had to drag their attention back to the lesson, but neither of them was really taking everything in. Occasional glances out the window told them that Gill had co-opted the free period staff to look for Abbie and Annie.

At the end of the first session, Annie still hadn't returned.

"Go away," Abbie insisted, when Annie came around the corner and saw her. She was trying, unsuccessfully to hide tears. "I hate everyone!"

"I don't," Annie countered. "Besides, I heard some of what Gail was saying to you. She was being beastly – just because you wouldn't dance to her commands."

"It's all my father's fault! He expects me to do exactly what he says, and he as good as said I'm not to buy lunches for anyone anymore."

"Well, why should you? How often do they spend money buying for everyone?"

"We took turns," Abbie protested. "I had to take sandwiches for lunch today."

"So? I do that all the time."

"You would! You're a charity case."

"I prefer to save my money for other things I want."

"Like what?"

"Like an IPad or a new laptop."

"Tell your Dad to buy one for you."

"And he says that what I have still works well so I don't need a new one."

"I tell Mum what I want and she gets Dad to get it."

"I'm not like that. Dad says you appreciate things more when you have to save for them. Besides, while he earns good money, with us having to move so often, a lot of it goes on that."

From just nudging Abbie as they sat together, Annie knew Abbie was avoiding the real reason why she had run off from her friends. Still, ranting about her father was helping.

"We should head back to where we are meant to be," Annie suggested. "The bell will go soon."

"I'm not going back to class."

"You'll be in trouble."

"I don't care."

"What will your Dad do if you are?"

Abbie clamped her mouth shut, then blurted, "He said he'd make me change schools. I'd say good riddance to this one."

"You can't mean that! Changing schools mid-term is awful, I know."

"It has to be better than listening to Gail and Helen."

"Believe me, it's not."

"You don't know everything they were saying! And what they have been putting on line about me."

"I probably don't want to," Annie guessed. "But you shouldn't let them bully you like that."

"What can I do? The more I want them to stop, the worse they are."

"Talk to a teacher about it, or the school nurse."

"The nurse is only good for physical stuff," Abbie argued. "I might be feeling sick right now, but it wasn't from the sandwiches I ate. And if you are worried about being in trouble, you don't have to stay, and you didn't have to follow me."

"I wanted to know you were okay."

"You're the only one then. And I am not even sure I deserve

to feel okay."

"You didn't deserve what happened."

"You know nothing! You should have heard what my father said. He blamed me! Just because I ran off. Gail reckoned I was lucky not to get raped and left for dead, and I would have deserved that."

"They're all wrong!"

"But I did run off from the hotel. And I was starting to think it was a bad idea, but I didn't want to go back. Then I spotted Wanda, and I took that as an omen. None of the loiterers dared even look at us when she was around."

"Wanda?" Annie queried. The name wasn't all that common.

"Someone I met doing that asinine community service, and she's in trouble now, because of me."

Annie wasn't sure what to say then. She knew a lot about Wanda, but it was confidential. Finally, when the bell had stopped chiming, she said, "You don't know that."

"I do. I saw her on the news. Her being put in a police car — handcuffed. I also heard Dad on about her to someone."

"If she wasn't involved, the police would let her go. So where was she when they took her away?"

"Probably near the place I went to."

"Then she can't have abducted you."

"Dad reckons she was involved."

"He was there, was he?"

"No, of course not. Anyway, I don't expect you to understand. You made friends with Kemple and he's one the police keep watching."

"And they've never found anything to charge him with."

"Maybe they have now. Gail said they had."

"How would she know? Except that she was probably talking to the Logans. They put that idea about and admitted they were making it up."

Annie had managed to put her worry about Martin aside until then. "Why do you dislike him?"

"My father warned me off him."

"More fool you, when you ran off because of something he said."

"I never said that!"

Annie realised that she had picked that up from her shoulder just touching Abbie. For a moment she thought of pulling on thicker gloves, then decided to 'take them off'.

The sensation she felt then, desperation, frightened her. Twice before, Abbie had run off, and had ended in trouble. The second time, worse than the first. *What if she did it again?*

"I read something, or heard it said, 'Don't get mad, get even'," Annie blurted. "I reckon, if Gail and the others are being so nasty, and don't act like friends, you should ignore them, as if it was your idea to ditch them."

Abbie emitted a strangled snort. "I've got the perfect revenge, but it's not for now. And I don't even intend to tell them later."

Once again, Annie had a mental image, and she recognised the two men Abbie had been with – her dad and Maude's trustee. Before she could censor her tongue, she said, "Are you really Gabrielle Hartley?"

"How do you know that?"

"I..."

"You did that freak thing again!"

"I...yes, sorry."

"How'd you even know?"

"I found a birth certificate, the one you lost. I slipped it back in your locker when I realised it was yours. I mean, when I realised you'd had it."

"You little bitch! I was worried sick I'd lost it."

"Sorry! How was I to know it was yours, at first."

"Well...don't tell anyone."

"Come back to class," Annie countered.

"You can go if you want. I said I wasn't."

It was back to that. Annie tried to argue, but Abbie was adamant.

"Ladies?" Gill's pompous voice made them both tense and look around. "I believe the bell for class went quite some time ago. Do you think yourselves too knowledgeable to be there?"

"No," Annie said in a very low voice, as she glanced at Abbie.

"Well, let's all come back to my office. You can tell me what you were arguing about."

"We weren't arguing," Abbie muttered. Gill ignored her and gestured towards the admin building. She turned her scowl on Annie as if implying, "This is your fault."

In the admin building, he had them wait outside his office whilst he went to find someone.

"Who is Miss Opie?" Annie asked in a whisper.

"Senior Mistress," Abbie said, then added, "You don't want to be on her bad side, either."

"Oh! Surely she will understand that I was checking you were okay."

"That depend upon what Gill tells her."

"What's his problem?"

Abbie shrugged.

"Are you going to tell him why you didn't go in at the bell?" Annie asked.

"It's none of his business."

"Well, it is, really. He's responsible for all the kids while they are here."

"Don't you start!"

"I'm not. I am just going to say I was worried about you."

Abbie forced a grin. "Yeah, I was upset...reaction and all."

They both heard the two sets of footsteps approaching and stopped talking.

"Okay, in here," Gill directed. He waited for the two students and the other teacher to enter, then walked in and around to his desk. The other teacher stayed standing next to him while he sat.

"This is coming to be a habit, Miss Jamieson," Gill began.

"I don't understand," Annie blurted, surprised by the comment. "I haven't missed any classes before this."

"This is the second altercation you have had with Miss Carson."

"We were just talking," Annie protested. "Abbie had been upset and I was trying to get her to come back to class."

"That's all very well in theory, Miss Jamieson," Gill told her. "Had you thought of going to your teacher?"

She hadn't, but she said, "I didn't know where to find Ms Sutton."

"Aren't you meant to be in her class now?"

"Well, yes, but —"

"And you could have asked to see Miss Argent."

"Who's that, Sir?"

"The school counsellor," Gill stated. She had the feeling he thought she should have known.

"I didn't know there was a counsellor," Annie admitted.

Miss Opie spoke up. "How long have you been here?"

Annie looked at her. "I started here this year, Miss."

Miss Opie nodded, and then confronted Abbie. "And why didn't you ask to see the counsellor, Miss Carson? I am aware you have had a rough few days, but that is why we have a counsellor here to help our students."

"I don't want to talk about it!" Abbie blurted. "I'd be okay if everyone would just pretend nothing happened. I's none of anyone else's business anyway."

"If it starts to affect your school work or attendance in class, it becomes our business."

"So, what were the two of you talking about all this time?"

"Stuff," Abbie told him.

"I was trying to get Abbie's mind off the beastly stuff some people were saying to her," Annie explained.

"And you weren't trying to find out all the salacious details yourself," Gill suggested obliquely.

"I didn't have to!" Annie said, and stopped herself from saying she had helped find Abbie. "What little they had in the news was enough for me to know it wasn't likely pleasant."

"I was under the impression," Gill said thoughtfully, "that you two were not all that friendly."

"So? I certainly don't hate her. That was in the first week of term, and you made a point of us learning more about each other. Now, well, so what if we don't hang out together. I saw she was upset and wanted to help."

"I think Miss Argent is much better suited to do that. So I will make an appointment with her for you, Miss Carson. Tomorrow. I will give your homeroom teacher the details."

"I don't want —"Abbie began to protest.

Before Gill could pontificate further, Annie said, "You should at least try her. Someone impartial, with no preconceived notions."

Abbie considered that and subsided. "Well, okay then."

Gill began to scribble something, and then passed a piece of paper to Abbie.

Abbie glanced at it and scowled. "Can I go?"

Gill shooed her out, Annie began to follow. Miss Opie stopped her.

"Annie, perhaps I can have a few words with you?"

With a final glance at Abbie's retreating figure, she said, "Okay."

They went onto a nearby office and this time, Annie was allowed to sit down.

"Your concern for your class mate is commendable," Miss Opie said as she sat behind her desk. "I think, though, it would be best if you let us help her now. I think her friends would be the best ones to help her through this."

"Her friends!" Annie restrained herself from yelling, "They

were the ones who got her upset today. Asking horribly intrusive questions, calling her horrible things, and not just today. They had a lot of nasty insinuations on Facebook too."

"Those are quite serious accusations," Miss Opie warned her.

"Well, it's true! Even on Friday when I was helping the SES and the scouts look for her phone, her friends were saying Abbie brought everything on herself."

"I will have a word with Abbie's teachers," Miss Opie promised, but to Annie it felt like a brush off. "Her father called us and gave us a brief rundown of events from Thursday when she went missing to Sunday when she was found. He asked us to keep unwanted attention from her."

Two things occurred to Annie, the first being the incorrectness of, 'On Sunday when she was found.' The second was how they hadn't kept unwanted attention from Abbie.

"So I will ask you to leave Abbie be."

"What?" Annie took a moment for the words to sink in. "I wasn't badgering her! I was trying to help! Anyway, we usually sit together for Maths."

The teacher merely listened and said nothing.

"So, what does that mean? I can't even talk to her?"

"I don't mean you should shun her," Miss Opie explained, as if Annie was slow witted. "However her father thinks it best that only her friends are with her."

"He's wrong, but if that's what he wants. I will stop bothering to care about her. Can I go back to class?"

"Yes, but you will have a lunchtime detention tomorrow, for being out of class today."

She felt the effect of that statement in the pit of her stomach. *It wasn't fair!*

She bit her lip to stop herself blurting that out. Instead she managed to say, quite steadily, "Well it is a small price to pay for being sure someone I like is okay. It won't happen again!"

As she stood to leave, she saw the teacher's expression. Miss

Opie must have sensed it as a rebuke, or defiance, but didn't know what to say. Whatever, Annie had no intention of shutting Abbie out of her life.

The bell between periods went as Annie was getting things from her locker. She moved to join Naomi and Karen to go to history. When their looks asked her silently, "What happened?" Annie just said, "Later."

Gail was nearby, being treacly nice to Abbie while in Ms Sutton's hearing.

"What are you doing here, Kemple?" Gail didn't try to be subtle. "Why did they even let you out? Heard you were involved in Abbie's trouble."

"You heard wrong!" Martin said coldly. Gail was taken aback by the fact he had spoken at all, let alone that his expression verged on a snarl. "And if you must listen to my cousins trying to sound important know it alls, be prepared to be pulled down to their level."

"You can't speak to me like that!"

"I just did, but you shouldn't make up lies to spread around." Martin walked off before Gail was able to articulate a return insult.

Gail, turned around, but spotting Annie heading for the lockers, moved that way. "You'd better keep a leash on your boy toy, Jamieson."

"You need to keep one on your tongue," Annie retorted in a quieter voice. Gail's face turned red, at having two of her usual victims facing her down.

"You going to make me?"

"No. I don't care that much about you. In any case, you damn well know that Martin was with the SES and scouts all Friday morning. So how could he possibly be involved in Abbie's trouble? He doesn't have a car, so don't start sounding off with blatant lies."

"Or you'll do what?"

"Nothing. I won't have to. The only people you could have got that nonsense from are people you are not meant to be in contact with."

Gail's expression turned to a scowl. "What about the police and ambos at Kemple's place?"

Acting as if it were news to her, Annie asked, "When was

that?" She tried to hide how her muscles had tensed up.

"Friday? Saturday? Sometime."

"That was over two weeks ago," Annie forced a sarcastic tone. "Whoever told you that should check their facts."

"Well, where's he been these past few days then?" Gail demanded triumphantly.

"Sick," Annie lied.

"That's probably what he told you, Charity Case. He doesn't want to lose the only girl still deluded about him."

"Deluded? I think you are talking about yourself."

Annie stalked to her locker, but Gail wanted the last word. "Kemple will find out that people know about him!"

When Annie kept her back to her, Gail shoved her into the lockers as she was crouching to get her books.

"Gail!"

Ms Sutton's severe tone drew everyone's attention. "You will apologise to Annie, right now!"

After a stubborn pause, Gail said, "Sorry, I slipped."

In a low tone, that Annie just heard, their teacher told Gail, "I want to talk to you after homeroom."

"What was that about?" Naomi asked, having just arrived.

"Gail trying to make trouble," Annie told her.

"About what?"

"Martin."

"What was she saying?"

Annie gave her an outline, but kept her voice low so their nearer classmates couldn't hear.

"That's ridiculous. He couldn't have been involved."

"He wasn't," Annie said staunchly. "I can't say the same about his father and his mates, but I know some things that she doesn't. It's just people trying to get him in trouble and I wish I knew why. They take one detail, and make a story up. I don't know why everyone seems to hate him."

"I wouldn't say hate," Naomi decided. "Until this year, he wasn't ever really sociable, and he got downright taciturn after Abbie dropped him last year."

"I'd say that was her father's doing," Annie said without thinking. She didn't have actual proof, just a couple of memory flashes from Abbie.

"Yeah, probably," Naomi considered. "Let's get to class."

Annie glanced at Martin when he came in just after the bell. His expression betrayed nothing, and he didn't look her way. He went to the first vacant seat and turned his attention to the front of the room where Ms Sutton was talking. She could see Gail glancing his way and occasionally nudging Abbie. It made her wonder if Abbie had let slip where she had been found. Though, if she had, surely Gail would have betrayed that fact. And, if she had, she can't have mentioned how it had happened. In any case, people all thought she'd been found on Sunday.

There had been little information released to the media, Annie knew. She had read the papers and watched the TV news. She actually knew more than the general public, and Martin had trusted her with the truth of his absence. She already knew his cousins had tried to cause trouble by making up things. She hoped that the situation that David had orchestrated would shut them up. All anyone might have noticed was Martin being in the city police station. How could they know what for?

It wasn't fair, Annie thought to herself. Martin had just started to loosen up, to be his real self, and now this. He'd gone back to saying very little at school, not even acknowledging her existence. Well, she didn't feel hurt by that. She had a good idea of the reason.

Even when they were on the way to school, he was quieter

than he had become. In spite of his belief that nothing could be proved against him, and his gratitude to David for getting him a lawyer, he had seemed dejected. He wasn't encouraging conversation with anyone.

When the class was told to read a chapter of the text, before answering questions, Annie couldn't concentrate. Gail's comment that people would find out about Martin, worried her.

What if Gill found out, or heard the lies being put around. The Logans would only have to cast aspersions in Gill's hearing. Somehow, Tom and Gerry Logan had an in with him. After all, he had come to the police station on their behalf, on the first day of term. They had mentioned a case of drugs. Well, an exaggeration, but close to the truth, even if only a fraction of the whole truth. Gail had to have listened to their lies, probably before David had seen them.

Oh how she wanted to be able to prove to everyone that Martin wasn't involved – but he had been thrown into the middle of it. She wasn't going to reveal Martin's secrets. He trusted her, and she knew he wasn't the sort of person everyone else at school seemed to think. The full story would come out eventually, but many wouldn't hear of it and still think Martin a bad sort.

Still, she really wanted to know why people were trying to denigrate Martin. There seemed to be no reason. She had sensed that Gill disliked him, from when she had spoken to him on the first day. Where had that come from? His reputation? If he heard of Martin being charged and on bail, what would he do?

She felt Karen nudge her and realised that everyone else had started answering the questions. She picked up her pen and tried to concentrate. She glanced at Martin and he seemed to be working hard. If he could, she could.

Ms Sutton met them in the small classroom near the staff room. She wasn't smiling.

"You've both got work to do?"

"Yes," Annie said. Karen had told her what to expect and she had come prepared.

"No," Abbie said. "I missed getting some of the work. It's probably at the post office in NSW. I am trying to get up to date, by asking my teachers."

"Have you the first lot of questions about the set text?" Ms Sutton was referring to the book for English.

"I have one lot," Abbie said, glancing at Annie. "Was there more?"

"Yes. I will see you get a copy later. Do you have the book here?"

"Yes."

"Then keep reading that. Annie what are you doing?"

"I was going to work on an Italian assignment."

"Alright, get onto it. I will be back later, and will expect to find you working. I am disappointed with both of you. You are amongst the students that I least expected to skip classes."

"Annie didn't have to come after me," Abbie blurted.

"No, she didn't. It was her choice. She could have left you alone and not given you more grief."

Annie opened her mouth to protest, but didn't. Ms Sutton was watching Abbie, not her.

"She wasn't" Abbie insisted.

"Oh? That's not what I was told."

"When old Gill found us –"

"Mr Gill to you, Abbie!"

"Alright, Mr Gill…found us, she was telling me to come back to class. I didn't want to."

"And why was that?"

"Because..." Abbie stopped what she wanted to say and finally said, "I had wanted to be alone. I wanted people to act as if nothing had happened to me."

"Your friends would have been worried about you," Ms Sutton suggested.

"By wanting to know everything? By telling me I deserved it all?" Abbie's voice rose in pitch. "I told them I didn't want to talk about it. Miss Argent said I shouldn't have to if I didn't want to, since they wouldn't understand. I wouldn't have even told her anything, except Annie was right. She wasn't critical of me, she helped me see some things differently."

"So why did you go after her, Annie? You two aren't all that close."

Annie had a lot of things she could have said, but stuck with the simple truth. "I wanted to be sure she was okay."

"Why did you think she wouldn't be?"

That was a question she didn't want to explain. She didn't want to tell their teacher things Abbie wouldn't want her to know. Yet the deeper answer was older than her acquaintance with her classmates.

"Someone needed to," Annie said, meeting her teacher's eyes. "Two years ago, when I was at a school in Brisbane, there was a girl in year 7 who killed herself. It turned out she was being bullied at school, and even more so on social media. Her friends claimed to be unaware of it, and maybe they were, but I heard some of the comments Gail was giving Abbie. Anyway, since Mr Gill insisted we got to know each other better, I decided I like Abbie, and if her friends weren't going to help her..."

"Someone had to," Ms Sutton finished.

"I told Miss Opie that having detention was a small price to pay if she was okay!"

"You feel deeply about this."

Annie nodded. "My school last year had a zero tolerance to

bullying policy. I reckon all schools should. I'd do the same thing again, if the situation arose, and even if I get rewarded the same way – because I knew I did the right thing."

"So why didn't you come and get a teacher?" Ms Sutton asked, interested.

"I didn't see any, and I wouldn't have been welcome at the staff room, I would probably have been told I was hysterical, or didn't know what I was talking about, or it wasn't my concern. I thought I could help, and if I couldn't and I was really worried, I would have gone for a teacher. Abbie just needed a friendly presence. She has more sense than a lot of people."

Ms Sutton looked back at Abbie just as she closed her gaping mouth.

"And I wasn't trying to break up any friendships, just make an extra one," Annie insisted, referring back to the altercation with Gail that morning.

"I would like to think on what you have told me," Ms Sutton admitted. "I do need to be elsewhere now, so I expected you both to work."

They both opened up books, and Annie set her Italian assignment in front of her, and her lunch beside her. Ms Sutton had closed the door, but this room had large windows that looked out into the corridor.

They were sitting on opposite sides of a six person table, one at each end, and if they spoke softly, they didn't think they'd be heard.

"I'm sorry I was rude to you yesterday," Abbie said, out of the blue.

"I'd forgotten," Annie said, accepting the apology.

"I'm sorry you got detention too."

"I did that. Ms Sutton was right about that."

"Would you have done it for some kid you didn't know?"

"Maybe, if I had heard them being bullied."

"Is that how Gail sounded?"

"Yes."

"She'd always like that."

"I'd noticed." Annie didn't want more trouble for talking, but Abbie seemed to want to.

After a while, she said, "If I think something, while holding something, and then give it to you, can you tell what I thought – using that freak gift of yours."

"I don't know if it works that way."

"Can I try something?"

"If you want."

Annie turned her attention back to her Italian assignment, while Abbie dug into her pencil case and took out a short plastic ruler. Then, while looking to be reading, she held the ruler.

"Here!" Abbie said, just before sliding the ruler down the table to her. Annie stopped it with her arm, the tentatively touched it. Abbie stared as Annie felt her face go blank.

She didn't hear voices, but oh, the emotion was intense, and it took her time to sort it out.

"Well?" Abbie hissed.

"Your father got you really upset," Annie began, but she stopped, as she heard the door opening. She repeated the statement in Italian, not looking at Abbie, so it would seem she was practicing something.

It was Miss Opie, checking on them. She merely glanced at them both and retreated.

Abbie muttered something that sounded uncomplimentary.

"Abbie? Call me after school. Okay? I really don't want more trouble just now."

"I can't. My dad will be checking on all my calls, emails and all."

"So?"

"He said not to talk to anyone but my friends."

"Oh?"

"Okay, I like you, but he doesn't know we are sort of friends."

"So, you aren't allowed to make more friends? Doesn't he remember you had tea with me a couple of times?"

"It's not what you think. Its…he thinks people will try to take advantage of me."

"Why now?" Annie couldn't help asking. Then she touched the ruler again, and more images came – older ones. They were related to visions she'd had the previous day. Knowing some things about Maude Hartley, she guessed the answer, but school was not the place to discuss it.

"Didn't the police give you back your phone? The new one?"

"How did you know about that?"

Annie put a finger to her lips. She was watching Gill stride past the classroom. Abbie spotted him too, and finally decided to keep quiet.

Annie went back to her assignment, but her eyes kept straying to the widow and the corridor beyond. She had just finished the last of her sandwiches when a loud thump on the door startled her. The door opened by itself, and she heard Martin's voice. Looking up, she saw him trying to shake off Gill's grip on his arm.

"I haven't done anything wrong!" was what he'd said.

Gill's reply was equally clear. "We will discuss this in my office."

Episode 23

Hostile Intentions

Chapter 1

"Annie!" Abbie hissed loudly after her first two attempts got no reaction.

"What?"

"Now is not the time to rush after Kemple to help him."

"I know that!" Annie wanted to though, and didn't need her class mate to add, "You don't want Gill on your case because of him."

The words seemed to be an echo of David Davis's advice, the "Don't try to contact him," warning. Even that morning, Martin had said, "Don't worry about me, okay?"

She couldn't help it though and wondered if Martin had kicked the door open on purpose, as a heads up. He knew she would be there today.

At the lockers after last bell, Annie heard Abbie ask, "Do you have skype?"

"No. Why?"

"We could talk that way and no one would know what we said."

"Would I need a web cam?"

"No," Abbie assured her. "Why don't you set up skype and send me a blank test when you have?"

"Okay," Annie agreed, just as Gail shoved her aside.

"Oh! Sorry! I just wanted to be sure Abs was okay." Gail oozed the fake concern.

Annie decided that Ms Sutton, or someone, had spoken to her.

"Good of you," she retorted sarcastically.

"I reckon you're poison right now, Charity Case. First you chum up to Abs, and things happen. Now things have happened to Kemple. I heard he's been suspended...indefinitely. You'd better watch out, they will be looking at you next."

"Well, I don't have a guilty conscience," Annie spoke over her shoulder as she returned to her locker. "Do you? Been talking to your boyfriend again?"

"So what if I have?"

"So...if that doesn't bother you, why should I worry?"

"What do you mean?"

"I mean, if you get found out, I won't care."

"If I want to talk to him, I will. Who's to know?"

A new voice spoke before Annie could. "If you boast about disobeying a legal requirement, Gail, you can expect trouble," Ms Sutton warned.

"I was only saying, if I wanted to," Gail said quickly, then moved away.

"Abbie, here's the last worksheet for the book, and some for history and Maths," Ms Sutton handed a folder of sheets of paper to her.

"Thanks," Abbie told the teacher, and she put then straight into her pack.

Annie waited for her to leave before finishing at her locker. Ms Sutton stayed nearby as the last of the other students left.

"Annie?"

"Huh?"

"A word before you go?"

"Okay."

They moved back into the classroom.

"I heard what Gail said to you. Was that why you were provoking her?"

"That was just a mild warning. She was trying to upset me,

but I don't listen to people who make stuff up, or repeat lies, just to be the centre of attention. They are only belittling themselves."

"She wasn't lying about Martin Kemple though," Ms Sutton said quietly.

"He told me what happened," Annie admitted. "Can I ask what you were told?"

"That he has been charged for a serious offence and is out on bail."

"So why does he have to be suspended?"

"It's school policy," Ms Sutton said quietly.

"The policy stinks! Sorry, it isn't fair," Annie blurted. "It seems like everyone is trying to force him to be no better than his father. He's trying to be better. Why else would he be trying hard to do well here? Is anyone even going to bother sending him work so he doesn't fall too far behind?"

Ms Sutton hesitated before deciding. "I will see what can be arranged? Are you volunteering to take work to him?"

"Are you going to tell me I shouldn't?"

"Do I need to?"

"No, but probably not for the reason you would tell me if I said I would."

"What reason do you think I have?" Ms Sutton asked.

"Because of what everyone around here seems to think of him. Because his father was lucky never to have been in prison and has now crossed that line?"

"You have only known him a few weeks," Ms Sutton pointed out.

"So? Not once in that time have I felt uncomfortable with him. He has never tried to come on to me, or even spoke rudely. He volunteered to help the scouts at their new building, and I know how he reacted to what they found there – he found there. He also helped look out for Maude Hartley. If he's a stand offish loner here, I'm not surprised. It's probably so he doesn't get hurt."

"You are full of surprises, Annie. So what is your reason for not going to his place?"

"Because I know what went on there last weekend and was asked not to talk about it by Detective Kelly. He also said I might not be safe if the people trying to get at Martin saw me. Otherwise, yes, I would insist on taking work to him."

"I see," Ms Sutton said gently. "I overheard Abbie saying something about Kemple's place."

"She wasn't going to say anything!"

"If you know what's going on, surely you realise that continuing to see Martin outside school —"

"No! Not you too! Martin could not have had anything to do with Abbie's disappearance. The police know that!"

"That wasn't what he was charged with."

"No, they found drugs in a bag he dropped. And that was a blatant frame up."

"Annie, you can't know that."

No way would she mention her freakish gift and how she could pick up things from people. Few people would believe her.

"Martin and I were with the scouts and the SES from early Friday to about midday. We walked back, and I left him at his place. He'd bought lunch and was going to go straight in to eat it. I remembered something I wanted to ask him, and as his phone was flat, went back. It was only a matter of ten minutes when I got back, but my dog found the bag with his lunch kicked under a bush in his driveway. He wasn't there."

"There could be..."

"Lots of reasons?" Annie interrupted and finished the sentence. "Well, DC Kelly didn't consider me hysterical, when he came. Lucky was yapping frantically at the garage door. I know what they found there, it wasn't drug related, and had not been there late the night before when Martin gave Kelly the key there to look for something. Someone was trying to get Martin in trouble."

"Do you want me to explain this to Mr Gill?"

"No way!"

"Why not?"

"Like I said, DC Kelly told me not to talk about what was found. I just wanted you to know Martin isn't bad. And, not meaning to be rude about Mr Gill, because I haven't known him long, but I know he doesn't like Martin, and will be even more against him. I don't think he will consider Martin innocent until proven guilty. Anyway, the police are not giving out a lot of details about things, and I think that's to catch all the people involved with the events Martin got dragged into. So the fewer who know, the better."

"I commend your loyalty to your friends, Annie, but I will add my advice to stay away from Martin's place and take a different route home, if there is one."

"Yeah, alright."

"Good, now if you can spare a few minutes, I'll give you a copy of the next section of English work. You can scan it and send it to him."

"Okay. I can do that."

Annie took the papers, and had the feeling that Ms Sutton wasn't against Martin, and the 'keep away' idea had come from Mr Gill.

Martin mentally bit his tongue to stop himself yelling back at Gill. He wasn't going to listen to anything he said. His first protestation of "I haven't done anything wrong here," was met with, "Perhaps not, but it is school policy to suspend students who have been charged by the police. We are expected to uphold the reputation of the school."

He could argue with that, to a point. They had expelled Jordan, but let Adam and Tony back. They had both been before the courts, like Abbie had. Gill would emphasise the degree of 'bad' and he couldn't argue about the amount of drugs that had been planted on him.

As if reading his mind, Gill said, "I understand you were found with drugs in your possession." His tone was severe and his eyes the colour of grey gun metal.

Gritting his teeth, Martin said, "No! That is not the case." He mentally added, '*technically, anyway.*'

He had dropped the bag and run off before being caught. "The bag they were in was not mine, nor did I know what was in it. The local police are aware of my movements from early the day before, and when that information is presented in court, I expect to be exonerated."

"Of course you will want that," Gill agreed. "However, if the police arrested you, they would have felt they had a strong case. If, as you say, there is no evidence, with your movements known, they would drop the charges."

Martin felt sure that Gill wanted to know all the dirty secrets, but he wasn't going to oblige. There were things he'd been asked not to discuss. "It's not that simple," Martin tried again. "My being framed is a sideline of an ongoing investigation. They don't think I'm dangerous, or likely to start selling drugs, or they wouldn't have given me bail."

"You still had the nerve to come here whilst under suspicion," Gill accused.

"I haven't deliberately done anything wrong," Martin tried to insist. "I came to school, because that is where I am meant to be. I didn't expect you to let me use that as a reason to stay away."

"You should have thought of that before doing whatever you did."

"You don't even know what happened, Sir!" Martin emphasised the 'sir' as deliberate insult.

"Why don't you explain it to me?" Gill invited.

"I am not at liberty to do that," Martin said truthfully.

"Convenient. However, I want you to clear out your locker, and go home until your exoneration is public knowledge."

"You can't do that!"

"I can. It is, as I stated before, school policy."

"What about innocent until proven guilty?"

"We at Bellfield College have a duty of care to the other students," Gill pontificated.

Other students? Yeah, but not him, Martin thought angrily.

"And I will insist that you keep away from the school and the other students."

"Can I at least have work sent home for me to do? I don't want to fall behind."

"In your current situation, you have abrogated your right to be educated here."

"I have not!" Martin felt his face heating up. He wanted to yell out. "My fees have been paid for a full year. You are obligated to educate me."

"Mr Kemple, you will remove yourself from the school grounds within the hour. If you are seen on or near the school grounds after that, the police will be called. If you are reported near any of the students, the suspension may become permanent."

"You have no right to stop me seeing my friends outside school," Martin blurted, as he turned and walked out on the bastard.

"Kemple!" Gill called after him.

"I'm going, alright! That's what you've always wanted, isn't it? Well, you will be hearing about this!"

"Who will I be hearing from," Gill asked in a voice just above normal.

Martin heard him, but ignored the hint of a chuckle in the teacher's tone. He could just imagine Gill retreating into his office and grinning like the classic Cheshire cat.

Just trying to hold himself in check was putting his gut into a knot. He wanted to slam things, kick things, yell obscenities, and call Gill all the horrid names his father had ever used on him. The bastard knew he was an emancipated minor. Probably knew that his father was in jail. He probably believed he had no one to turn to, or to speak up for him.

And he didn't. He couldn't get his mother to talk for him, or his step uncle. They had totally cut him off. Not that he wanted to go crawling to any of them. He thought of David, but Gill would not accept an American, who had only known him a month, as an advocate.

It wasn't fair! By rights, he could represent himself, but he was still a kid. Only fifteen. No one believed kids his age. Gill would assume he would lie to show himself in a good light.

His class were in their home room, and he didn't want his disgrace to be known, so he emptied his locker quietly. When he was done, he closed and locked it. Damned if he would act as if he wasn't coming back. Not that anyone in his class would care if he didn't come back. Well, except for Annie, and maybe her two friends. And damned if he would stop seeing Annie. She was the only person who liked and believed in him.

He shrugged his laden pack onto his back and slipped around the building to head for the back gate. Once he was away, he let out all he was holding in. Gill's unfairness was at the top of it. The bastard was acting like he was a habitual trouble maker, or criminal. Jordan, and Tory Michaelson had done worse things than he had and only this last time had they been suspended or expelled. How had Gill learnt of the charges against him anyway?

And what was that crack about being publically exonerated? Unless he was a celebrity, the media wouldn't proclaim the innocence of an innocent 15 year old non-entity. Besides, from what David had told him, the investigation was on-going and it might be months before it was finalised.

By the time he had power walked home, his anger was turning to depression. He was on his own. He was still just a kid. With no one to stand up for him. Now, his one avenue of hope had been slammed shut in his face.

Inside his house, he let the heavy pack drop to the floor, and he kicked the door shut. He swiped his sleeve across his eyes, then stalked to the kitchen. In the pantry, there was still a six-pack of beer – his father's, but now it was his. He'd kept it for guests – grown up ones, but now he took one. It wasn't cold, but he didn't care. It was all he could think of to deaden the intensity of how he felt. He had never really liked the smell of the stuff, but he forced the can full down. It only made him feel worse -sick and miserable.

He recalled the advice of eating as well or you would feel more intoxicated. He felt in his pocket for the half sandwich he'd not eaten when Gill dragged him off. He left it there, if he ate it he would probably be sick.

His house began to feel like the cell he had been kept in for almost three days. He abruptly turned back to the front door, and almost ran to get out, but didn't forget to lock up. Then he began to walk. He was too tensed up to stroll, he needed to tire himself out, or heaven help anyone who crossed him.

With no particular destination in mind, he just walked, finding himself on one of his usual routes to work, but watching only the path in front of him.

"Martin!"

The sound came from the car he was just passing.

"Huh? Oh, David. What are you doing here?" Martin looked around and realised where he was.

"I was going to ask you, however, you need to get scarce, fast!"

"Why?"

"Scram! Don't look around. Duck down the next street and keep going. GO!"

"But..."

David came out of the car and moved to give Martin a push in the right direction, and in doing so smelt the beer breath. "Martin?"

"I'm going."

Martin realised that he wasn't thinking properly, and concentrated on 'duck down the next street'. He only had to pass six houses to get to the corner, but if he kept going straight, Carson's house was only another six houses past the street. Just around the corner, his momentum evaporated, and he stopped to try to recall the rest of what he had been told.

Don't look around. Too late, he was doing that as he recalled the direction. He saw a car, he thought he should recognise, drive past the street. The delay in comprehension gave him the impetus to "keep going". The car had stopped in Carson's driveway, and he recognised Kelly and Kaspersky getting out. The question of why they were there was eclipsed by the surety that he didn't want them to see him and ask why he wasn't at school. They knew about his horrid three days, and probably had orders to keep tabs on his movements. They wouldn't be impressed if they thought him drunk. He didn't want to hate them, but he was finding it hard not to hate all police because two had not believed him.

His mind cleared a little, and he made for the park. He didn't go far in, just to a shaded spot under a tree where he could drop down and hold his spinning head.

David waited until after Carson had gone off with the two detectives before starting his hired car. He turned at the side street and kept an eye out for Martin. The teenager should have been at school, not wandering around. Plus he had claimed that he never drank alcohol – something was wrong.

On a hunch, he parked near a cut-through to the park. It was just a strip of grass between two houses. He considered that Martin might be heading for the shop where he worked. He didn't have to go that far however, before he saw the sprawled figure and ghosted up. When he wasn't noticed, David sat beside him and waited.

"How long have you been there?" Martin asked after a slight sound had woken him.

"Not long. I was enjoying the quiet, and watching other people go about their business."

"Were you still watching Carson?"

"Sort of. I had to do something and I wanted to see what he did now Abbie was back and he'd taken her to see the Hartley lawyers."

"Are you supposed to tell me that?"

"Probably not, but you and Annie are Maude's friends."

"But how is he involved with the Hartley's?"

"Certain information was received that revealed he was the father of Maude's girls."

"Then that means-"

"Apparently, Abbie is one of the twins."

Martin, still a little beer addled, could only stare, but his own problems had been pushed from his mind.

David went on, "How do you think Abbie would feel about that?"

"I don't know how to put this politely…"

"It's just you and me," David pointed out.

"I really don't think Abbie will be impressed to be told she is the child of a mad woman, or even a simple one. Carson has encouraged her to be a snob, like those friends of hers and I like to call them the Hells Angels. They all have this 'I'm better than you' attitude. Would that be why Delaney took her?"

"That's a question he isn't answering," David murmured.

Martin's slow mind had only got as far as 'Carson fathered Maude's kids' but that thought recalled another. "So that's why Maude thought he looked familiar. Why didn't she recall his name?"

"Because she nick-named him Wally."

"Do you think he really is the father of her girls."

"It's likely, but Tyrell has sent off DNA samples to be sure." David kept the oddity about the girls' DNA to himself.

"Can I tell Annie this?"

"Maybe later."

"She might already sort of know," Martin considered. "Abbie ran off from class yesterday, upset about something. Annie went off after her. They both had detention today."

David merely shook his head.

"Abbie acts like she doesn't like Annie, but I think she does but doesn't want Gail to know. Annie might have picked something up – but she rarely says anything about those flashes."

"I don't blame her," David commented. "Do you think Abbie would be likely or tempted to talk if it is proved she is a Hartley?"

Martin thought about it. "Last year…I would have said she would. Now, I don't know. Mostly she's acting the same, but I didn't expect her to go and check on Annie's dog, and a few other things. Lately, she's been behaving real stupid, like going off with Adam, and running off last weekend."

"Have you any idea how she's been since she got home this time?"

"Not really. I know her so called friends have been poisonous towards her. I heard that much this morning before Gill threatened me."

David's head snapped around. "Threatened about what?"
"The usual. Implying he knows things about me."
"We were not giving out any information."
"You got your friend to ring about me being away," Martin reminded him.
"Kelso wouldn't have said why, but maybe he assumed things. Your cousins had heard stuff too, possibly from the Michaelson character."
"I reckon Gill has a soft spot for my cousins."
"Oh?"
"Yeah. On the first day of school, when I was dragged to the police station, Gill was there, speaking up for them."
"Interesting. Maybe that is the connection. I put a scare into your cousins, who claimed they'd been making things up. Anyway, how about I buy you some lunch. I need some and I think you need to try and soak up some of that alcohol before some official type thinks you're drunk."
"Yep. I don't need that."
"Okay. Just let me make a phone call."

Martin's mind registered that he was talking to a hospital about Wanda. When he finished, Martin asked how she was.
"She had an operation today. It was deferred from Monday. It's why I've been so twitchy. But it's over, she's in recovery and I can see her this evening. Why don't you come in too?"
"Will it be alright?"
"If I say so, yeah."

By the time they'd finished a meal from Mc Donald's, David decided that Martin was much less muddled, and much calmer.

He offered to drive him home, but Martin suggested a spot about half way between there and the school.

"Gill told me to stay away from the school and the other kids, but I damn well don't think he has the right to dictate that I can't meet my friends."

"I don't think he has either. Tell me what he was saying to you."

That made the short trip pass quickly. David made no comment, but Martin thought he was remembering it all.

At the chosen spot, a bus stop with a shelter, David remarked, "I gather your friend will come this way? Will she know you aren't still at school?"

"Yeah. I made a bit of a commotion as I was being dragged past the classroom where she and Abbie were. Kicked the door open. Wanted to do more than that. Anyway, I reckon Gill will have told Annie to avoid me and my place, or get Ms Sutton to do it. So if she does, her alternate route home comes out just along a bit."

"Just keep a low profile," David advised. "I've had words with Gill before. He does come over as full of his own importance. Try not to rile him."

"He's usually the one who starts things."

"Let's drop that subject, okay? What say I pick you up at 7.30?"

"Yep, okay."

Annie headed home, walking faster than usual, since she was later leaving. She wondered if Martin was waiting to meet her somewhere. She hoped so. That morning, she'd had the feeling that he needed a friend, and he didn't seem to have many.

Seeing him up ahead, just before where she would have to turn off to go a different way home, made her smile. He began to grin when he saw her.

"Mrs Sutton says she will send work home for you," Annie said as soon as she was close. "She gave me some English stuff. Actually, I'm meant to scan it and email it to you."

"Was that your idea?"

Annie nodded. "I don't think she is against you."

"Gill is though," Martin said, scowling. "He was practically rubbing his hands with glee."

"Ms Sutton said you were charged with something serious and were on bail." It wasn't quite what he'd said that morning.

"Yeah. I was. I didn't want you to worry. It wasn't a little amount of drugs, it was enough to be a commercial amount."

"So that's why you were keeping away from me?"

"Kinda. Did Ms Sutton know details?"

"I don't think so, or just the result."

"Gill found out somehow."

"You didn't tell him?"

"Of course not! All I did was have someone send a message to say I would be away from school a few days. The person was not going to say why, and I trust his word."

"Was that David?"

"No. The ex-cop he is working with."

"David did let me know that you were okay, and said not to try to call you."

"Good of him, and he's right. I'm glad you don't ask questions."

"Well, I guess you don't want to tell things, and I'm not meant to discuss things, even with you, so fair's fair."

"Not quite. I know they found Abbie in my garage, but she'd not been there long. And I know your mutt had a lot to do with that. Thanks."

Without thinking, Annie reached out and gently squeezed Martin's hand. "At least you have calmed down since lunchtime." She decided to change the subject.

"Well, I stalked off. I didn't want to go home, and I didn't want to be anywhere near Gill any longer than I had to be. I was too agro. I went home first then decided to walk it off. Met David. Rather he saw me and told me to make myself scarce."

"How come?" Annie sensed this was something he did want to share.

"He was parked down from Carson's place. Watching, I expect. But just after I ducked down the next street, a police car went past. I edged back to look and it stopped outside Carson's place, and he went off with them."

"I'm glad he's not my dad."

"Yeah. I'd have yours over him any day."

"Oh! Do you know anything about Skype?"

"Where did that come from?"

"Oh, Abbie thinks it might be a way for us to talk without her dad realising. It seems that he only wants Abbie to talk to her existing friends."

Annie explained what she had been told, and what she had sensed from Abbie.

Martin scowled. "If he is really keeping close tabs on her phone usage and internet, he must know what Gail has been saying. Surely though, he's not such a bastard as to condone that."

Annie shrugged.

"You'd better not run off after her if she goes off again."

"I told Miss Opie that I'd have to decide at the time."

"I bet she didn't like that."

"I don't know. She did look at me funny when I said getting detention was a small price to pay for being sure Abbie was okay. I told Ms Sutton the same thing, that I'd tolerate detention because I knew I was right."

Martin laughed. "And I thought you were a nice, quiet-"

"Heard the one about having to watch the quiet ones?"

"No. But I will remember that in future," Martin chuckled.

"I wonder why David was watching Abbie's dad," Annie went back to the earlier subject. She didn't want to discuss getting detention. She hadn't told her Dad yet.

"He said it was because he was too twitchy to be sitting around at the hospital."

"Huh?"

"Wanda had her operation today. It was deferred from Monday."

"Oh, right."

"Told me I could visit her tonight if I wanted to. Something about keeping her quiet. Why don't you see if you can visit too? Maybe your Mum or Dad would drive you."

"I will see what they say, but Mum is likely to be too tired. If I don't go, will you say hi for me?"

"Okay."

They reached the end of the detour, and Martin grinned before heading home. Annie went on with a lighter heart. Martin seemed a lot less tense now.

David picked Martin up in the evening, on his way to the hospital. Annie had rung to say she wouldn't be coming, that her Mum thought it wouldn't be a good time.

"Are you sure she won't mind?" Martin asked. "Me coming, I mean."

"You will help keep her quiet," David said again, and Martin wondered what he meant.

"But you will be there."

"Yes, but I also need to go and talk to someone."

"And you can't say who?"

"No, but it's all about finding out who took Abbie and why."

"They have Delaney, Crane and my father."

"Yes, and the two Wanda took out in Footscray, but we still have questions as to why."

"Do you think Delaney has something against Carson?"

"We know they knew each other," David revealed.

"That's not a very good character reference," Martin noted, being tactful. The idea that Carson knew Delaney gave him a bad feeling. "How much longer will you be staying? Don't you have kids to get back to?"

"They are fine, and enjoying the chance to get to know their younger aunts and uncles. I have been assured they are having a ball. We talk to them over the computer."

"I'm glad you were here still," Martin admitted, sincerely. "Earlier, I was feeling pretty depressed."

"Glad to help. I know what it is like to be young, alone and with no one to turn to."

"Well, however, I appreciated you listening."

"And I appreciate your understanding of why we can't hurry your court case."

"Annie has Ms Sutton on her side and got her to agree to sending work to me."

"Well, if that isn't enough to stop you getting bored, let me know. I'll give you a link to an on-line electronics course."

"Really? Would you?"

David chuckled. "Alright."

At the private hospital, David went first to the reception desk to show his ID and check where Wanda was. She had been put in a different ward when she had been brought back from the recovery room.

Martin went tense as they went through a security check, but David only had to say who his companion was and he was let through.

At first glance, Martin thought Wanda was still asleep. She had an oxygen mask on and was lying on her side. He stood back and watched as David went close and leant over to give her a kiss on the cheek.

"How are you feeling?"

The voice that answered didn't sound sleepy, but it said, "Dopey."

"They knocked you right out then?"

"Yeah, but I'd told the specialist to talk to Doc Wallace. Hopefully, I won't feel like rampaging around this place, later. I have to keep the mask on to flush out the last traces of the gas."

"I have to go chat to someone, but I will be back later. However, I brought a well-wisher."

Wanda moved slightly and spotted Martin. "Oh good, someone who can talk to me."

"Can't David?"

"No. He's not allowed to tell me a lot of things."

Martin just shook his head. "Annie sends her regards too."

"Tell her thanks, I intend to act on all the good wishes I can get." Wanda turned her attention back to David. "Well? Shoo! Go and do what you have to do." Her husband grinned and went out.

"So, how are you holding up?" Wanda asked, moving carefully to see him better. "Oh, do come and sit down!"

"I'm okay, but Gill kicked me out of school."

"Pompous ratbag!" Wanda muttered.

"Annie talked Ms Sutton into getting work sent to me."

"Well, that might help keep you out of mischief."

"David said he'd give me a link to an online electronics course."

"Oh, so you are into that, are you?"

"Well, I want to get into communications."

"Interesting. I learnt electronics at the same time as I was learning to by-pass security stuff."

"What school taught you that?"

"One I hope you never go to," Wanda expressed. She decided to change the subject. "Is Abbie back at school?"

That got Martin talking about his day and Annie's trouble.

"I would like to treat your Mr Gill to a lesson," Wanda said conversationally. "But, it probably wouldn't be tactful, and he is only filling in. How did you get on with the proper head master?"

"Mr Allen? He's alright."

"You know, I was thinking...in my much too commodious free time this week...about offering to teach some of the students self-defence. How do you think that idea would go over?"

"Are you fit enough for that?"

"Oh, don't you start! My arm's functional enough and in any case, I have a spare arm, two feet and a head."

Martin laughed. "I think it's a good idea. They might consider it as part of the PE curriculum. Would they have to pay you?"

"No. This would be gratis. However, depending on the degree of interest, I might have to draft in extra instructors, who might need to be paid something."

"Well, if the people interested have to pay something, that might limit numbers," Martin suggested.

"True. Anyway, I will have to see how things go here first."

"I think Annie has done some of that stuff."

"Has she? Hmmm..."

"What are you thinking?"

"Dastardly thoughts that I had better not share."

Martin found himself grinning. "So, how are you?"

"I was told the procedure went well. They had to realign the little bones in my ear. I have to behave myself, to let the bones fuse. After that, my hearing and balance should be back to normal."

Martin decided that for someone who had described herself as 'dopey', Wanda was fast getting over it. He was enjoying talking to her and learning fascinating hints about her past. She mentioned nothing about the events they were both involved in and he began to wonder about the secrecy and why it was needed. It seemed to be more than just because the events were being actively investigated. Annie had mentioned that Wanda was being a decoy or a distraction and that idea puzzled him. However, he knew he wouldn't get an explanation.

He had been with her half an hour when a tall man entered. From his attire, Martin assumed he was a nurse, for he was also wheeling a trolley containing the equipment for taking blood and making patient observations. The oddity was that the man had a mask on.

"Why don't you go get a drink or something while I endure this rigmarole," Wanda suggested.

Martin took the hint, and sidled past the man who seemed to be preparing tubes and needles for some sort of test.

Wanda noticed the man's mask and felt a prickle of warning. It was nothing like her usual sense of danger, but she didn't dismiss it. The man wasn't any of the male nurses she had seen before, but this one would be an asset in the security ward where she had been put. She shifted her position so that her good arm was free of the blanket. The doctor had warned her that she did not want to catch a cold, for sneezing would be very bad, until the bones had fused. The man's mask might just be a precaution.

She'd had three days of the hospital routine, so was surprised when the gloved hand took her wrist to check her pulse.

Normally they put the clip thing on her finger. The man's eyes were watching the clock over the wash basin, but the grip was firmer than usual and the other hand was fiddling with a syringe.

The details added up, and the last of the anaesthetic induced mental lethargy evaporated.

She twisted abruptly, freeing her other arm just in time to swat the syringe from the man's hand. It landed on the floor. He growled a curse and moved his hand to her neck, the pulling off the air mask and slipping his hand under it. There was no time to shriek a warning, but although the man held one arm, preventing her from using it, her other one hit him on the side of the face with nails ready to scratch. The hand over her nose and mouth increased its pressure, but Wanda forced her mouth open enough to bite, but began to feel the need to breathe, and felt herself blacking out.

In that last few moments of awareness, she mentally yelled and stopped fighting.

The man felt the woman's body collapse, and become limp. He removed his hand slowly and felt for a pulse in her neck. He felt nothing, and quickly moved the air mask back in place and fixed his own mask to cover where the bitch had scratched him. Moments later, he was striding away from the ward.

Martin, who had just emerged from a toilet, was nearly bowled over. He recognised the figure, but didn't see the face. The man made no apology, nor did he stop to ask if he was okay. Martin watched over his shoulder to see which way the man was going as he headed back to Wanda.

One look at her, caused his belly to cramp as he went to the door and yelled towards the nurses station, "Help! Here!"

He went back in and gently shook Wanda, getting no reaction.

Somehow, David arrived ahead of the med-team. "What happened?"

"A male nurse came to do observations and I went out to get a drink. He came out and practically knocked me over."

"See if you can find where he went. Tell the guard to put a call out." David spoke as he was doing his own observations, checking breathing and pulse. He immediately began to force air into his wife.

Martin stepped aside to let the med team in before running out. He had a very good idea of the direction the man had gone.

David couldn't say if Wanda had been in the odd 'out of body' state or if she had really stopped breathing. Either way, he was relieved to feel a tendril of thought directed at him. Simply, "Get the bastard."

He didn't mind, then, being eased out of the way so the professionals could help her. A few minutes later, they confirmed that she was breathing on her own and her pulse was strong. In a moment when the med team moved apart, he spotted blood on Wanda's right hand.

"Can you get a sample of the blood on her hand? I think she marked the guy."

The doctor leading the team wanted to know what happened and David repeated what Martin had told him. The trolley the guy had brought in was still in evidence. "I am going to insist on a guard in here and I will go and see if Martin found where the man went."

No one objected. The staff knew who he was, and that he was on the Atlas Task force. They all wanted the impostor caught.

One of the security officers at the ward entrance went up to Wanda's ward, even though the chance of two imposters getting in was slight.

David caught Martin as he came back, breathless. "He got into a taxi. Must have ducked in somewhere to ditch the scrubs, but I am positive it was the same guy."

Immediately, David drew out his phone and dialled Kelso. "Which cab company?" he demanded of Martin.

When Kelso answered, he ordered, "Get onto the yellow cab company and find out about a fare that just left the hospital. I will explain later." He ended the call and asked Martin, "Did you get a good look at him?"

"No. In the room he was keeping his face averted, and in the passage, I only had a glimpse – he was fiddling with his mask. How's Wanda?"

"Her? She'll be okay."

Martin breathed easier, even as he watched David's intent expression.

"Do you know who it was?" Martin asked.

David shook his head. He wasn't going to air his speculations in Martin's hearing. Instead, he said, "He made a major mistake. Wanda scratched him. Head back to the ward, will you?"

Once Martin was out of earshot, David called Kelso back and gave him a full report and requested an update on Jeremy Carson's movements. The description Martin had given, didn't fit Carson, except in being tall and male, but if Carson had been switching identities all his life, he'd be a good actor and used to changing his appearance. Mainwright had just begun to share what he knew when Wanda's mental call had sent him running.

He hoped the local police would move in on Carson soon. The incident today, if it was indeed Carson as Wanda thought, revealed he had a vicious deadly side. If he showed signs of an injury, they had a reason to get a DNA sample for official use. Then they could compare it to that of Robbo and Thea.

Carson couldn't have been thinking, even if he'd had the brazen effrontery to pass the security guards. He must have wanted to prevent her from accusing him of anything, or testifying against him. The question was, did he believe he had finished her? He can't have expected Wanda to fight back as she had.

David managed a faint level of mirth. If the devil couldn't handle his mate, what chance did an amateur like Carson?

Martin hovered outside the ward until the crowd of nurses and doctors felt it was okay to leave. One doctor remained inside and he was doing something with Wanda's hand.

"You can come in, lad," the doctor invited. "She'll be okay, thanks to you. Did you see what happened?"

"No. I went out when the man came in. I assumed he was there to check her vitals and stuff. She didn't think it odd. What did he do?"

"Failed to smother her. I am told he'd not have got anywhere, if she hadn't been slowed by the residual anaesthetic. Even so, I think she did twist out of the way of something. I found a damp patch on the sheet. It might have come from a syringe."

"Why isn't she awake?"

"Could be a few reasons. Give her time. Are you a relative?"

"More a friend. Possibly a very distant connection," Martin admitted.

"Well, if you are going to be sticking around a while, you can natter at her as if she's awake, and when that husband of hers comes back, tell him to call me."

"Okay…"

Martin paced the room while he waited. On the third repetition, his eyes were on the floor and he spotted a syringe, under the little wash basin, right against the wall.

"Doctor?"

"What, lad?"

"There's a syringe on the floor."

The doctor twisted immediately and looked where Martin was pointing. "Don't touch it, lad. Just stay there."

The doctor went back to carefully scanning Wanda's arm, as David slipped quietly into the room. Two nurses followed him, carrying the necessities for an infusion.

One asked David, "Did you stop the drip that was running."

Martin glanced at the drip bag beside the bed and saw it was still pretty full. He heard David admit that he had, adding, "I couldn't be sure nothing had been added there."

He watched one of the nurses drawing the curtains around the bed, and David being eased out. From his expression, he guessed that David was worried by something about his wife's condition.

"David?" Martin ventured.

David forced his attention from the closed curtain. "What's up?"

Martin pointed to the syringe, but didn't need to warn David not to touch it, even when he crouched down to examine it better. All that was obvious was that the plunger was half way in. He wished he knew what David wasn't saying, and what had occurred to him to make him stand up quickly and ask to be allowed inside the curtain.

Only parts of the quiet conversation were clear.

"The syringe is still half full..."

"Looks like she blocked him and knocked the syringe away..."

"Will the drip be checked for drugs? And the sheet?"

"Naturally."

"You have found so sign of an injection?"

"No. It seems that the missing amount went on the sheet."

"I think, some did get into her bloodstream. Could it be absorbed through the skin?"

"It may be possible. We will have a better idea when the tests are done. We will be doing everything your doctor friend recommended. Once I've finished here, I will see to having her moved upstairs."

"You will let me know what you find?"

"Yes, lad. And you will tell us what you expect?"

"I did already. If she has some metabolites, she will be hyper. Depends on the drug."

"No problems, lad. Now, there's nothing more you can do here. Why don't you leave the young lad here and go back to finish what you came to do. Then if your wife decides to give us trouble, you will be free."

David growled and emerged from between the sections of

curtain. He headed for the door and Martin followed. Just outside the door, there was now a police guard. David moved a little way down the passage.

"I hope you will keep this business to yourself," David said.

"Yes, but I can't be sure Annie won't pick something up from me."

David seemed to be thinking. "I hope she doesn't. She's still young and innocent."

"She's learnt a lot about the real world this past week," Martin told him. "But I understand what you mean. I don't know how she would react if she picks up that I think Abbie's dad tried to kill Wanda."

"Did you recognise him?" David asked, intently.

"I only had a quick glimpse of his face straight on and then he looked away, but I think he did recognise me. Oh, the guy didn't look like him – being blonde, not black haired, and having glasses, but his profile looked similar and Carson was the first name to come to my mind."

"I suggest that you don't volunteer the idea, and if Annie picks up on it, say it's unlikely."

"But it could be?" Martin persisted.

"Can you think of a good reason?" David challenged.

"Well...no. Will you be checking out Carson?"

David grinned faintly. "Kelso is on it. Someone will look him up, try to see if he has any scratches. If so, he will have to explain them. Where did he have skin showing?"

"His arms were bare and a bit of neck. He was fiddling with the mask he'd had on when he came out."

"Okay. Leave things to the police and a vengeful Kelso. When they let Wanda be, go and just talk to her. Then let me know when they decide to move her."

"Okay." It seemed that David needed to be elsewhere, when he wanted to stay. Keeping his wife company was a way to repay David's trust and help.

Episode 24

Not So Clever

<u>Chapter 1</u>

"Who are you really?" Robbo demanded, more as an attempt at a growl. He didn't want to move from the comfortable position he had finally achieved.

David introduced himself with his official ID, but quickly added, "I'm not here to accuse you of abduction or anything else. I did want to be sure you were recovering. My partner did what she could for you until the paramedics arrived."

"You mean the chick who came in with our little sis?"

"Wanda, yes. I think she also told you Thea is staying where we are?"

"I wouldn't mind being able to talk to her," Robbo suggested.

David spotted one of Kelso's cards on the bedside cabinet. He picked it up, showed Robbo and said, "Call the number on that and ask for her." He nudged the room's telephone closer to the bed.

"Thanks. So what do you want?"

"I understand that you believe that Jeremy Carson used to have another name."

"More than one. What are you interested in him for?"

"His daughter appears to be the missing heiress to a sizable fortune."

Robbo snorted, then grimaced. "Sounds like him."

"Why don't you tell me about your father – that's who you think he is."

"Yeah, but when we confronted him, he denied even knowing his own flesh and blood."

"How sure are you that he is your missing father?"

"Damn certain. He knew me alright. His face gave him away, then he blanked it."

"How different does he look now?"

"Well, he has black hair, not reddish brown. But he still has a scar, just to the left of his nose and another on his chin, on the right side, just as it curves under."

"Is the eye colour the same?"

"Yes, slightly green speckled brown."

"What year did he leave you?"

"2002," Robbo growled. Then he went on to tell what his mother, self and sister had found when they had returned from a holiday. "He'd cleared out everything from his bedroom, office and everywhere. Anything personal. He'd even been through mum's stuff, and ours. The rest of the house seemed like it had been professionally cleaned all through. Plus there was a sale sign out the front with the sold sticker."

"It was your mother's house wasn't it?"

"Yeah, she inherited it, but when she married him, she let him take control of all the finances. Mum thought she still had a say, until we checked all out bank accounts. Mum tried to stop the sale, but he'd made sure she couldn't."

"Are you aware that the chances of getting any money back is slim?" David warned.

"He's still stinking rich, isn't he?"

"I don't personally know," David admitted. "I only know he pays a high rent for the house he's in. Tell me how you found Carson."

"He wasn't so damned clever! He'd pinched a bunch of photos Thea had taken with her instamatic, but the negatives had fallen out, and he missed them, and Mum had a tiny photo of him in her purse. I hadn't known back then that mum had been convinced he was having an affair and was looking for clues. When she was dying, she told me she had been keeping stuff that he hadn't found. That house had lots of odd little nooks."

"Did she hire a private detective at any time?"

"She never mentioned it if she did. Anyway, she had a metal box she kept behind a sliding panel in her bedroom…" Robbo stopped what he was saying for David had inexplicably taken on a blank expression, stood up and put his notebook and recorder on the chair. He practically ran from the room, saying only, "I'll be back."

Staring at his visitor's odd behaviour, he wondered what had caused it. The guy had been dead keen to hear all about how Jeremy Carson had once been Justin Mainwright. By listening intently, he deduced some sort of flap, and the muted call for a MET team to go to a nearby room suggested an emergency, but the David guy had run off before that.

Robbo realised he must have dozed off, for he woke when David returned. He studied the other man's face and saw his tense expression. "What happened?"

Although David shook his head, he said, "It seems my partner made someone feel threatened, and he tried to silence her."

"Wanda? Is she okay?"

"She will be. She'd had an op earlier, and was still a bit dopey. She still tricked the bastard, and scratched him. He might think he succeeded."

"I was wondering, before I dozed off, about your interest in Carson." Robbo decided to drop his deliberate belligerence. "You hinted he might be planning to pull another scam. Was that what the task force was looking into?"

"No, their targets were put onto Carson by one of the men we wanted. Do you know a man called Mickey Delaney?"

"No."

"Well he knows Carson, and he is the man who stabbed you."

"Has he been caught?"

"Yes, Wanda caught him." David decided it was close enough

to the truth. "I am authorised to get a statement from you about the abduction business, but right now I am interested in Carson. I would like to get back to the things your mother had."

"That, yes. You know I think my father's utter and total betrayal of her, caused her illness. We were left with nothing. We moved from a large expensive house into a hovel. Anyway, before she died, Mum showed me what was in the box. Some of the stuff was his. A ring, an expired driver's licence a paper one that expired in 1996, the odd bank statement and tax assessment slip. I don't know how she got them because our father was careful to shred all old documents like that. She even had some of his hair – like what you take from a hair brush."

"That could be useful. We could get a DNA test done on that."

"Even if it's twenty years old?" Robbo questioned. "But you'd still have to get a sample from the bastard to compare with it."

David's face creased into a grin. "There may be ways."

"Bastard put a restraining order on us." In his annoyance, Robbo moved injudiciously. "The lawyer we got on our side can't do much more."

"What do you hope to achieve by revealing him?" David asked.

"Wanted to get a share of his money and ours back. Failing that, to make his life hell, like he made ours."

"So, was that all you found?" David asked. There had to be more if Robbo had traced Carson

"No, there were some envelopes – one addressed to a Jacob Hillier, one to Jeremy Carson and one to a Jarryd Stillman. We checked those names – found birth dates on all, but also a marriage certificate for Carson dated 2002. The very year he whacked off on us."

David wanted to yell, "Yes!" at the mention of Stillman and

Hillier. He only allowed himself a satisfied smirk as he asked for details of Justin Mainwright, his mother Dolly Mainwright, and various significant dates. Then everything Robbo and his sister had done to trace Carson.

"What's made you happy?" Robbo demanded.

"The name Stillman has turned up in a side investigation," David admitted.

"Something crooked?"

"Maybe more like a coffin nail, or another piece of evidence. Now, would you be willing to bring everything you have to my current boss, Kelso? We would copy or photograph what you have, and you would keep the originals."

"What would you be doing?"

"Initially, probably repeating the searches you did, but Kelso is ex-police and still has contacts. He might be able to dig deeper and in more places than you or I could."

"And if you find dirt on him, will he be charged?"

"If we have enough to prove him guilty, yes. It might only be for recent activities, as some things have a statute of limitations. However, if we can link him to other schemes, it provides a precedent."

"I guess that's something."

"Are you up to talking more?"

"About Carson? You bet, mate!"

Robbo felt the twinges in his repaired gut but the chance to air the dirt on Carson made them seem trivial.

David went on, "Okay, I am deliberately separating your 'civil' disagreement –"

Robbo snorted. "Hardly that!"

David grinned agreement but went on, "...from recent events. Can I walk you through the events from when you saw Abbie Carson at the Hyatt Hotel on Thursday evening?"

"You know about that?"

"I've spoken to Abbie."

"Does the old bastard know?"

"Yes...but only the bare facts put into a police statement."

"I'm beginning to like you, mate." Robbo grinned.

"I'm after the truth," David stressed. "Facts that can be verified, and it might mean you admitting to your intentions. Carson has tried to accuse you of abducting his daughter."

"She came to us!"

"Yes, but Delaney coming and attacking you, then taking off with Abbie, puts a different light on things. He didn't take her directly back to Carson."

An evil gleam came into Robbo's eyes. "Is the little sis okay?"

"Yes, except for having to listen to her father's ranting."

"What can I tell you?"

"Start with, how did you know she was at the hotel?"

"I didn't. Not until I saw her wandering around the shops. Then I asked a favour of the desk clerk. We're mates. He helped me get a job there. He confirmed the sis and her mother were staying there. I kinda got an idea of how the mother must be. Anyway, I work in the kitchens, and when someone had to take the meal trolley up, I was nice and handy."

David listened, recorded all, and made occasional notes. Robbo had taken the hint and was being very candid. When he'd seen Abbie, he'd mentioned he'd rung Thea, a fact that could be verified to fix the time neatly. Just as his usual shift clock off proved when he finished work, and potentially there might be a way to determine when he used his electronic transport ticket.

"Yeah, I called Carson when the little sis turned up. To gloat, you know. I could have said it was so he wouldn't worry and all but I don't like him enough for that. Oh, I know it was stupid, now."

David gave him a different perspective. "It is also a way to check when she arrived there. It can be related to when other events were instigated."

"You going to explain what you mean?"

A head shake was his answer. "Once you were put out of the game, you can't be accused of later events. That is what needs to concern you. Go onto what happened after Abbie and Wanda arrived at the house."

Much of what Robbo said then was already confirmed by Wanda's statement, and the one Kelso took from Thea. David used what they had said to elicit more details. When he felt he had explored the events fully, he stopped the recorder.

"I will have a statement typed up," he told Robbo, "and have it brought in for you to sign. Make sure you read it properly first in case you need to add or amend details."

Robbo noticed a figure hovering at the door to his room. "Who do you want?"

David turned. "Oh, Martin. You were after me?"

"You said to let you know when they are moving her? You didn't answer the text I sent."

"Hey, I know you! You were the kid I spoke to at the little sis's school."

Martin took a closer look at the patient. "Oh, yes." He wanted to drop the subject, as he didn't want to think about school.

"I'll be in touch," David promised Robbo. "You can contact me through Kelso if you need to."

"I'll ring later, to talk to Thea, oaky?"

David nodded, and turned to leave. Robbo tried to find a comfortable position to rest, but even when he did his mind was still racing – full of possibilities of punishment for his bastard of a father.

"I didn't interrupt anything important did I?" Martin asked.

"No, we were pretty much finished. I didn't want to tire him out any more." David was walking quickly to where a bed was being angled out of Wanda's room. The orderlies stopped when they were in the passage, to let David talk to Wanda. Martin didn't hear what they said, just saw David's hand grip hers. He expected David to kiss her, but he may have decided it was too public. When the orderlies began moving the bed again, Martin pressed back against the wall. Wanda's face was white, but she saw him and raised her had to give him a 'v' for victory sign. The hand was noticeably shaking.

Something inside him relaxed. She was okay. Then he had doubts. She had not seemed to be hearing him while he was sitting with her.

"I can find my own way home if you want to stay here with her," Martin offered as they watched the bed pushed into the lift to go up a level.

"No, it's okay. I can't do much for her right now, as much as I want to. She'll be fine. I know that. So now I want to get the misguided bastard who thought he could get rid of her."

A nurse approached. "Mr Davis, I was asked to tell you that Senior Constable Heuser and his partner are on their way up."

"Thank you," David said before hurrying back to room Wanda had been in. "Wait out here," he directed before going into where the forensic pathologist was carefully bagging the syringe. To the pathologist, he said, "There is a police dog and his handler coming up. I don't know if they will be able to pick up the intruder's scent, but if the dog can get a scent of that compound, and follow it, it might be something."

"I will be here," the man promised and David nodded.

Martin recognised the officer and the dog, Rufus. They were the ones who had been at the scout house. It reminded him of how the bones identified as one of Maude Hartley's girls, had been found. That day had been pushed from his mind, but now it all came back. Carson was supposedly the father of that dead girl, and if he had guessed right that evening, Carson had tried to kill Wanda. The man was a callous bastard.

While David explained what he hoped to do – track the intruder's movements – the dog came and sniffed him, after sniffing David. He heard the officer tell the dog 'friend' each time. Then David let the dog and handler go in and he spoke from the door.

"The intruder stood this side of the bed, but the MET team were all around it."

Heuser nodded, as he told his dog the pathologist was a friend, and the pathologist handed Heuser a plastic bag with tissues in it. He explained, "The tissues have a trace of the chemical compound on it. I hope it is enough to give your dog a scent."

"Thanks. I'll try that if he doesn't pick up a scent he can use. Having others come in, makes it hard."

David suggested, "Martin has some idea of which way the man went."

"Maybe you could sniff the door frame near the gents down there," Martin pointed as he spoke. He bounced off the wall when he nearly ran me down."

Heuser gave his canine partner directions.

David held Martin back to give the dog time to sniff the passage. It seemed a good omen that Rufus turned in the direction of the gents without being directed. Heuser held him near there to let him have a good sniff before asking his dog a question. He received a faint woof, and then let the dog move on.

Martin confirmed that the man had gone left further down – exactly where the dog changed direction.

"I think he has the right scent," he whispered.

Rufus sniffed at a door, and Heuser opened it without using the handle. "Davis?" he called.

David looked inside. Rufus was sniffing at some fabric in a bag that was connected to an overturned holder.

"Martin? What colour did the man wear?"

"Dark blue."

"There's a mask in the bin, and gloves," Heuser said pointing to a bin for contaminated items. He had Rufus sniff there and understood the smell was there too.

"Do you have anything to bag these in?" David asked.

"When the discarded clothing, gloves and mask were in one of the spare bin bags, the dog was allowed to sniff further. He found a section of shelf of interest, but nothing was there.

"Okay, let's see if Rufus can follow the trail onwards from here," David suggested.

While following the dog once again, David asked Martin, "What was the man wearing when he reached the taxi?"

"Dark pants and a loose light grey jumper."

When the dog reached the foyer, David moved off to the reception desk where two detectives were talking to the desk clerk. They stopped as he approached and showed his ID.

"I just wanted to ask if there is a public phone near here, or a means to call a taxi.”

“No, Sir,” the clerk said. “Sometimes I will call a taxi for people, if they ask when I’m not busy.”

“Thanks,” David said before retreating.

The dog had gone outside, and Martin was waiting at the door. “Now what? They are at the place where the taxi picked the guy up.”

“Give me a moment.”

David rang Kelso and made a request for the receptionist to give a statement, and then went back to ask the woman a question about whether she had seen a man answering the description Martin had given him.”

The answer wasn’t helpful. The woman had probably been on a call or answering another query. Still, he thanked her again, and directed a question to the detectives.

“I have a bag containing clothing, mask and gloves that may have been worn by the intruder who attacked the woman on level three. Chief Superintendent Kingley wants it at the forensic laboratory as quickly as possible. Do you have a form for providing the provenance of the items?”

One of them did, and made sure all the details were given. The other went to request a forensic team to look at the room David specified, and would debrief Heuser when he returned.

David thanked them and shrugged for Martin to follow him.

“I think we can leave everything else to the local police. They will get onto the security footage and have what we found analysed.”

“I wish I could order the police around,” Martin murmured.

“If I didn’t still have that Task Force ID, I couldn’t,” David admitted. “The important thing is that the facts are found out.”

“I guess. What now?”

“More leg work. Are you bored yet?”

“Hell no! I feel like I am doing something useful.”

“Well, just remember to keep all this to yourself. I will aim to keep your name out of it."

"Except that I can identify the man who might be Carson, and if he is, he knows me."

"True, but the man in the ward and the one who you saw get in the taxi, did not look like Carson."

"That dog was amazing," Martin said, realising David's point.

"Yes. We can link the two men you saw, and we can identify the time and check if Carson's so far secret phone made the call for the taxi."

Once back at David's car, Martin finally felt he had a moment to think. "Why would Carson try to kill Wanda?"

"She has a knack for irritating people," David said neutrally. "Generally because she is right and can remember little details."

"But if he would do that, is Abbie safe with him?"

"For now. He thinks he has got away clean. He thinks we have no way to prove he has done anything illegal. Except that Wanda overheard him talking to Delaney. Even on that, he thinks she has been taken care of. Abbie is safe, because she is his golden goose."

"Why isn't that reassuring?"

"Because the ego-centric villain is showing he can be ruthless."

Whatever David intended was changed when his phone rang. He touched the Wi-Fi earpiece and listened intently. All he said was "Okay" before hanging up.

"Change of plans," David apologised, as he started the car and moved out into the light traffic. "I have to go back to Kelso's place, so I will just run you home."

Martin mentally shrugged, "Thanks for letting me help."

"Thank you for sitting with Wanda."

"I don't know that I did much. She seemed pretty out of it."

"She gave you the victory sign, so I think she was more aware than you realised."

"Will you let me help out again?"

"Depends if Kelso is about to chew me out for putting you at risk."

"You could say you are keeping me out of trouble."

"How are you managing at home?"

"Fine."

David glanced at him, but said nothing. He didn't think the answer sounded all that positive. Well, he couldn't do any more just then. Kelso had been most emphatic.

"David, good. Get inside," Kelso greeted him.

It seemed prudent to obey without asking questions. He was glad he had when he saw the visitors in Kelso's lounge room. His reading of the Assistant Commissioner and Chief Superintendent Kingley, told him their business was serious.

Kingley gestured him to a seat. "How's Wanda?"

"The operation went well."

"And tonight's events?"

"If she hadn't still been addled from the anaesthetic, that guy would have been tied up in his own ego!"

"But she's okay?"

"She will be. I asked for her to be transferred to the psych ward. The person tried to inject her with something. Seems she knocked that away, but some was leaked onto the sheet and she may have absorbed some of it through the skin. The doctor did not see any sign of a needle puncture. Until the stuff is analysed, I can't tell how she might react. She wanted to be contained if she did have a reaction."

"I instructed the hospital to imply she was moved away for an autopsy," Kingley told him.

David didn't disagree but decided to test their logic. "Do you think that is needed? Why not have her in a coma?"

"Because it will make that person overconfident," Kingley said.

"Do you have any idea who it might be?"

"Do you?" was the immediate counter.

"Yes," David admitted. "But he was carefully disguised. I don't intend to make unprovable accusations."

Gordon Forrest, the Assistant Commissioner said succinctly, "Jeremy Carson."

David saw Kingley's face tighten and wondered if he had been quizzed about his friendship with Carson.

"Yes, Sir," David agreed. "I'd taken Martin Kemple with me - to keep Wanda amused while I had things to do there. The man barrelled into him, and that was Martin's first thought."

"He knows Carson?"

"I've heard he was going out with Abbie Carson last year, but Carson warned him off. A different view was that he didn't want penniless boys interested in his money."

"That boy is on parole for possession of a commercial quantity of drugs," Forrest provoked.

"Yes, Sir. But I don't believe it." David met the man's gaze and held it.

"Why don't you share your reasoning?"

Kelso nodded for David to answer. His face was serious, but his mouth was twitching.

David did as asked, impressing his audience with his recall of details and the connecting logic. When he finished, he let Forrest consider it all.

"You didn't point out that Carson prepared that case of cash. Do you think he put the drugs there?"

"I didn't know who had prepared the case. Nothing I have heard about Carson suggests he's into drugs. However, Delaney and his mate Pirelli, were. It is more likely that Crane put the drugs there while he was switching the money to another bag."

"So, if he didn't know about the drugs, why did he run?"

"Sir, the boy is only fifteen. He is trying to be better than his father, whilst continually being accused of wrong doing. I would say he was scared."

After a moment of staring at Forrest, David added, "I will

stake my reputation on his innocence.”

Kelso murmured, “His formidable reputation.”

Forrest backed down. “I am inclined to agree with you. Now, I have been getting summaries of events all evening. Each mentioning you. I would like to hear what you have been doing.”

Kelso stood up and walked off, he returned with a can of soft drink.

“Thanks, I think I will need that.” David hid a sigh.

He hadn’t had time to itemise the events into a coherent time line, so he told things as he learnt of them. Then he was quizzed by Forrest for over an hour. Generally he kept to facts, but when asked for his opinions, gave them.

Finally, Forrest was satisfied. “I understand you are compiling a time line of the activities of persons of interest.”

“Yes, Sir.”

“I would like to see it. When can you show me?”

“I will need to add today’s information, Sir.”

“Yes, that would be wise. I have some other reports to add. One from the taxi driver and the units watching Carson’s place.”

“Thank you, Sir.”

“So, I will see you at 2pm tomorrow. Will that give you enough time?”

“Plenty, Sir.”

“Good. See that you spend some time with your partner.”

“I will, Sir,” David agreed. He intended to be there when she came down from the hyper effects he knew she was currently dealing with.

Kingley rose as his superior did. “I will be looking Carson up tomorrow, and will try to discover if his face is scratched. Though it is likely he will have them well hidden. If the man you saw is Carson, he must be very good at disguising himself.”

“I believe he is,” David agreed. “I am beginning to wonder if the appearance you are familiar with is actually his real one.”

Kingley gave him a thoughtful look before departing.

"Hungry?" Kelso asked, once his visitors had gone.

"Yes."

"I'll get you something. And I think you are right about Carson. Thea will likely prove it for us once she can get to where Robbo has his 'evidence'. She recalls him having brown hair, not black, and wore it styled differently."

"It's likely. I know what Wanda can do to change her appearance. She has learnt all the tricks."

"Why didn't you mention that to Kingley?"

"Surely my hint should be enough?"

Kelso chuckled. "Well, we will see. Come and eat before getting into the reports Gordon left. They are in my office. I hope you don't intend to stay up all night."

"That depends." David grinned sheepishly. "I would have no success at sleeping for a while. I am picking up more than you would believe from Wanda right now, and it is making me twitchy. I need to be distracted."

"I am starting to believe it possible," Kelso admitted.

Eating did help, David decided, but getting into the reports worked better. As he added data to his timeline, he became even more certain that Carson was the one who had tried to silence his wife. The taxi that had picked the man up, had dropped him near Riverpark. None of the taxi companies had reported a pick up from near there, and the Uber dispatchers had nothing either.

The man either lived nearby or was going somewhere nearby or had arranged a different pick up method from there. Still, it was suggestive.

So far, Carson had not been seen coming home, but he could have snuck in from the adjoining street. It was possible Carson had suggested that route to Delaney. No one who knew Carson would think him likely to be so undignified…or likely to commit a murder.

David continued working through the reports and came to one that had him wanting to dance with glee. The officers watching the CCTV cameras monitoring Riverpark near the storage units, had reported a man with dark pants and a light coloured hoodie going near the unit hired by the mysterious Ben Stillman. There had been plenty of time for the man to have walked from the taxi drop off point to there. If it were Carson, he could have gone home to get a box of stuff. The hoodie had hidden the man's face, but he was a tall man. It was an odd time to be near the units.

"I can't assume it is him," David reminded himself. "That would be persecution…but the reports are documented facts."

He finished adding the new information to his spread sheet, and thought to check the recording from the listening device in place in Carson's house. It was movement activated, but had a time monitoring function. Since his last download, the only obvious sounds were from Victoria Carson, Abbie or the housekeeper. There was no suggestion that Carson was around. He was going to have to find a way to remove that device. If Carson found it, his lawyers would have a good case for harassment. Nothing he had heard from it could be used as evidence, but it had proven useful for getting ideas of where to investigate.

He had heard the old chiming clock in the hall announcing it was 2 in the morning when he finally felt able to sleep. The twitchy feeling had abated as well. He hoped Wanda had finally worked off the drug effect from the anaesthetic and was sleeping as well.

Abbie was more than ready to get back home. The afternoon, after the detention, had been as bad as the morning. Her friends, supposed friends, she mentally amended, were not helping her. Why couldn't they just drop the subject when she asked? She wanted to forget what had happened to her, not dwell on it.

She had been abysmally stupid, running off because of a casual remark her father made. What had she been worried about? He'd take her money, money she still didn't believe was hers anyway, and what? Leave her on the side of a road somewhere like an abandoned dog? Surely her mum wouldn't let him do that. She hadn't actually thought of that at the time – it was more that she didn't want him to get what he coveted. Today she had wanted to run and hide again, and didn't dare. Her father had warned her about getting in more trouble. Too many detentions might just make her dad mad enough to carry out his threats. But that had actually been the best part of her day. She had been away from Gail, who was, as Annie had pointed out, a bossy bitch. She realised Gail had always been that. Her dad was bossy too, she suddenly realised. Perhaps that was why Gail had seemed okay.

On the way home, she had given the automatic, "It was okay," to Mrs Buttrose's question of, "How was your day."

Annie and Gail were total opposites. Gail would not keep quiet about getting detention and would have been beastly to anyone who caused her to have one. And she hadn't bothered to find out if her friend was okay. Annie, who she had rebuffed over and over again, hadn't let that stop her. She had not once blamed her for being in trouble. Just accepted the result, because it was nothing compared to knowing her classmate was okay.

That reminded her of her intention to talk to Annie on skype. How much else had she picked up from that ruler? That was freaky. She hadn't even thought of her father's despotic tantrum when she had tried that experiment.

Mrs Buttrose merely offered to bring up a drink, when Abbie headed for the stairs to get to her room. She had received a 'thanks', and been ignored thereafter. The housekeeper didn't rebuke the girl for what was rude behaviour, because she felt her employer – Abbie's father – had been too harsh. She didn't dare say anything against him – it wasn't her place. She had Carson summed up by the end of the job interview, but she needed the job. Well, she had a little treat to take up to her with the drink, and she was sure it would not be mentioned. Such a tiny defiance was all she could do.

Victoria Carson heard Abbie arrive upstairs and emerged from her own room. She seldom slept with her husband anymore, and the room was her refuge. She went to her daughter's room and entered without knocking.

"Don't you ever knock?" Abbie demanded as she was changing from her school uniform. Then she noticed her mother's 'fluttering'. Victoria's hands were in constant motion, a sure sign she was agitated or worried.

"What's got you in a dither?" Abbie asked, less belligerently. She waited for the fluttering to stop, once her mother decided what to say.

"Jeremy went off with two policemen. He's been gone for hours!"

Abbie felt the news as a gut reaction. The first thing her mind came up with was, *I hope they lock him up!*

"Oh, Mum! Daddy doesn't need us to worry. He can look after himself."

"Oh, I know that, but I think they think he had something to do with your ... your bad experience."

Abbie suggested, "Well, usually, when things like that happen it's because someone is against the parent."

"Yes! That's what it must be. After all, Jeremy is very rich."

"Yeah," Abbie agreed, but she was reminded of her suspicions about him. She wanted her mother out of her room. "Was that all? I want to get started on something."

"Yes, I'm such a silly thing. But I was afraid they'd not let him back," Victoria admitted, reaching out to give Abbie a hug. Awkwardly, Abbie hugged back.

The visitation occupied Abbie's mind as her computer booted up, and she opened up skype.

Was her dad involved in her abduction? Ideas flitted through her mind. She had been sure he wouldn't like her knowing Robbo and Thea, whether they were her half sibs or not. But he hadn't been around when she had seen Robbo. But...her mum had seen him, and when she'd found her gone, the first thing her mum would have done was call her dad. Wanda had mentioned that her phone could have been used to track her, and her dad might have known where Robbo lived. Surely though, he didn't know criminals like Delaney?

Just thinking the name gave her shivers. Other odd mentions that she'd ignored, returned to her. Like, Delaney had been married to Maude Hartley, her supposed real mother. If her dad was her real dad and after the Hartley fortune, might not Delaney also be interested in it? He was her father for a short while. A very short while, Abbie told herself. That would make it more likely Delaney was behind it all. Made more sense.

Abbie went to get her books from her bag. An idea struck her. How did Delaney know where to find me?

That took her mind back to the original question, and the next question. What if her dad and Delaney were in it together? That the abduction had been arranged to get her back and to teach her a lesson.

Abbie collapsed onto her bed. If he had done that, then his ranting at her had been totally unfair and he would deserve to be locked up.

For a while, the prospect of her father being in jail was entirely satisfying, even though a little voice was telling her it wouldn't happen. Then another little voice suggested, *What if it does?*

She forced away thoughts of, "where would we live?" and "where would they get money from?"

"Daddy's rich. We would use his money," she told herself out loud.

Reassured, she opened skype, checked she'd had no contacts show up, and minimised it. When she heard Mrs Buttrose coming up the stairs, she checked the time. Annie probably hadn't even got home yet, and would probably want a snack too, and may have other things to do – like play with the pup.

It was after six when she heard her father's car pull up outside. The car door closed with more force than normal. She ran quickly to the window. He must be intending to go out again. Maybe he had a late client meeting. She had a glimpse of his face. He was scowling. That was not a good sign. She crossed to her door and cracked it open. She heard the front door open and close, again with more noise than normal. Then she heard her mum, venting her concern for him.

"No, Victoria, of course they don't think that. They wanted me to think who might have something against me. Disgruntled clients and such. Apart from those two scam artists, I can't think of anyone."

"But you were gone so long!"

"I wanted to do all I could to get the people responsible put away for good."

Abbie thought he sounded unruffled, but she recalled the scowl. He was acting now, for her mother's sake and would probably be extra nice to herself for the same reason, so she wouldn't worry and would stay sweet. He could try!

Abbie checked skype for messages, and quickly minimised it again. Just in case her dad came up to see her. For the same reason, she took out her maths homework and got started on it. There was still no notifications on Skype when she was called for tea.

Tea was like everyone was walking on eggshells. Abbie chose to keep quiet and let her mother chatter away. As soon as she could, she excused herself to return to her homework and check skype. This time she had a message, but she didn't answer right away. Her dad had mentioned going out, and she had claimed she wanted an early night. She had told him she had used her lunch hour to catch up on work. Well, that was true...and it had made her father smile. So claiming to be tired wouldn't be so surprising. Her brain needed to relax.

Her father had left before Abbie answered Annie's message. She didn't get an image, just heard Annie's voice.

"Abbie? Is that your bedroom? It's big."

"Yeah. Where are you? In yours?"

"Oh, that's right. You can't see me. I asked dad about getting a webcam, he said he'll see about it. Oh! I talked to David to ask about your new phone. Haven't heard anything, but he might not be able to do anything anyway. When Martin and I found it, Kelly took it. He's a detective from the local police station."

"David?" Abbie's mind went to the guy who had taken her statement. "Tall guy, good looking, blond?"

"Yeah. Do you know him?"

"We've met, He's some kind of police guy, isn't he?"

"He says he's a consultant," Annie told her. "He's American, obviously, but he had nearly finished the work he came here for."

"How did you meet him?"

"He and Wanda were around when Martin and I found Maude Delaney. You know, that was when they had that huge police operation in River Park. They aren't stuffy like the police."

"Wanda?"

"His partner, wife too. You know her, or do you? She was picked up by the police from where you went…" Annie's voice trailed off. "Abbie?"

"I'm here still. Yeah, I know her. I just hadn't realised what she was. I mean, she was doing gardening when I did my first stint of community service. I thought she was… well, nothing like a cop."

"She's not, but she really took to Maude that night we met. She knew how to connect with her. Not many people would bother, I think."

"Is Maude really mad?"

"No! She's nice. She just finds it hard to say what she thinks. Wanda says she's got more going on in her head than she can get out."

"I'm still not sure I want to meet her. I shudder to think she might be my real mother."

"Oh, I forgot that. Do they know for sure yet?"

"No. Didn't you pick any of that up when I gave you that ruler?"

"Only a bit," Annie said slowly. "I got all sorts of images, all in a rush, and I haven't had time to sort them out. But if you are Maude's daughter, she will be so happy. She's had a really rotten life and the paper said some of the bones found at the scout house were those of her other daughter."

Abbie shuddered. "I can't imagine that I might once have had a twin."

"You must have been separated when you were really young," Annie proposed.

"I am still finding it hard to believe they actually think I am the other one. Anyway, what else did you pick up?"

"Well, I saw you and your dad talking to a guy I'd seen talking to Wanda last Sunday. I mean, she didn't look like herself but it was her. She had a really painful arm. It was in a sling."

"Huh? Do you know what happened?"

Annie didn't answer right away, but finally said, "I think it was something that happened on Friday."

Abbie recalled thinking she had lost a day. Maybe she had lost two. "What day did your dog find me?"

"It was Friday, why?"

"Well...I was supposedly found on Sunday, according to the papers."

"Yeah. I don't quite get why they didn't let on then. But I was told not to discuss things."

"And I decided not to tell my dad. David took my statement Saturday night. So I lost two days somewhere."

"You probably needed time to recover," Annie suggested.

"Oh, I'm not angry. I reckon it serves my dad right for being such a jerk. My Mum was upset though."

"I got the idea they were trying to catch everyone that was involved."

"I don't think they have yet," Abbie decided to say. "My dad was talking to the police for most of the afternoon. Trying to think of anyone who might have a grudge against him."

"Well, you be careful," Annie suggested.

"I'm practically in jail here now, anyway," Abbie didn't try to hide her resentment. She forgot Annie could see her, and scowled.

"At least we can talk this way," Annie said to distract her. "Surely your dad will ease off soon."

"You don't know him."

"Do you want to try this again tomorrow?"

"Okay. You'll be my secret friend."

"If you like. I wish for your sake that Gail and the others weren't being so beastly."

"They'll get bored of it soon enough," Abbie tried to convince herself.

"Probably. But why don't you try to put them off balance by smiling at them when they just stare at you."

"What will that do? They will want to know what's so funny."

"Yeah, but they will have to talk to you to ask, and you don't have to answer."

Abbie laughed. "I don't know if I can pull it off, but I might just try."

"Well, we will still have a secret –you and me – that they won't know about."

When they finally stopped talking, Abbie decided that talking to Annie had made her feel less depressed. It was funny that she had also met David and Wanda. It occurred to her that Wanda must have been pumping her for information, but if she had, she can't have shared it with her dad. In any case, having her turn up that night, and coming with her, well that had been good. Except it seemed that the police now thought she was involved with crooks and she was in trouble. Or was she - if she was out and about on Sunday? But she had hurt her arm. Had that happened at Robbo's?

Maybe, but she was certain of one thing. Wanda had been concerned for her, and not at all critical like her dad. Most adults would have forcibly taken her home, if they did anything. Or if they were like the men she'd seen...no, she wouldn't think of them.

Abbie changed into her pyjamas before going down to get a drink. Mrs Buttrose, was putting the last of the clean dishes away, and told Abbie that her mother had gone to bed and her father expected to be home late. It suited her, because she still wasn't ready to sleep and had decided to listen to one of her favourite music CD's. When that finished, she was feeling sleepy, and ducked across to the toilet. On her way back, she heard the sound of the front door being opened and quietly shut and hurried back to her room. She had left her door open a little, and just as she was on the verge of sleep, she heard a thud and a hissed oath from downstairs. Curious, she waited a few moments then slipped out to the top of the stairs where she could look down to the hall. She was hearing an odd shuffling sound and edged out a bit further. Her father was on hands and knees, sweeping a mess of things towards him and putting them back into a box. On finishing, he stood and saw her.

She yawned widely and asked, "Was that noise you, Daddy?"

He said, "Yes. I knocked over a box. You head back to bed."

"Okay, Daddy." Abbie faked another huge yawn, and went back towards her room. She was, however, no longer ready for sleep. She had never seen her father dressed as he was, in track pants and oversized jumper. And, unless she was dreaming, her father's face was scratched.

Expecting her father to check she'd returned to sleep, Abbie got into bed, glancing at the clock. It was only a quarter to eleven. With her door wide open, she could hear more odd noises from downstairs. The big entrance hall created odd echoes that were audible in her room. She wasn't going to check, but she thought her father was going in and out of the back door a few times. She couldn't guess why, but about then she fell asleep.

Next morning, her father was dressed in a suit as usual, though he had a cravat style scarf instead of a tie.

Episode 25

Closing In

Chapter 1

David only noticed the message when he was leaving the hospital in the early hours of the morning. He'd managed a few hours sleep before heading in to see Wanda. She was over the worst of her after reaction but had agreed not to be in a hurry to get out. He was considering having more sleep, but Annie's question about Abbie's phone got him thinking. He knew she had her original one back. The one her father knew about. But the one Martin and Annie had helped to find, might technically be evidence. He hoped it hadn't been given back, and Carson had found it. He made a mental note to check it.
On arriving back at Kelso's place, he grinned. Inside, was the very person he needed to see. Not surprising, because Kelly was Kelso's grandson.

"How is she?" Kelso asked first.

"Over the worst. Have they had forensic reports on the compound yet?"

Kelly pushed at a folder. "The Sarge told me to bring it. I expect you will understand more of it than I did."

"Only if I have heard of the stuff before. Otherwise I will need to ask questions of the pathologist as to what class of compounds it fell into."

"I'll let you find that out and explain to my sergeant how it affected your wife. Meanwhile, I was told to check with you about young Martin Kemple's whereabouts. He wasn't home when we went to check on him.”

“I can vouch for him between about one thirty and three thirty yesterday. I found him stalking around in a right grumpy mood. The school, in their short sighted wisdom, suspended him. Gill said it would last until he was publicly exonerated. As if the media will care about such a minor delinquent.”

“Yes, I’d been told he was suspended. And warned not to talk to any of the other students at the school.” Kelly didn’t betray what he thought of that.

“And I picked him up from his place at seven-thirty, before I went to the hospital. Dropped him back at about ten-thirty.”

“Did he mention seeing anyone?” Kelly asked.

“He grumbled that he didn’t think Gill had a right to stop him talking to his friends. And I agree.” David deliberately avoided the truth. Martin likely had met Annie. To distract the detective, he went on to say, “Did you get told that he raised the alarm and got fast help for my wife?”

“No, but I’m not surprised,” Kelly admitted.

“If he needs a character witness, would you be willing to give one?” David challenged.

Kelly answered with a nod, and then stood to leave.

“One other thing,” David said. “That phone Martin and Annie found on Friday? It was Abbie’s, wasn’t it?”

“Yes.”

“Is there any reason why Abbie can’t have it back?”

Kelly considered. “I passed it on to the officer in charge of the abduction case. I don’t know if it gave any clues, but it might be considered evidence.”

“I know she has the new one her father gave her recently, but I would hate to think the other gets returned and her father finds out about it.”

“Are you condoning the idea of that girl having a means to duck out on her parents again?”

“I know she hasn’t shown herself to be mature and responsible lately," David admitted. "However, if her father is giving her no privacy, overseeing all phone and internet usage, and treating her like a prisoner in her own home, he is not preventing rebellion, but practically guaranteeing it."

"Speaking from personal experience?" Kelly asked with raised brows.

"Next best thing," David said with a fleeting grin. "And right now, the only friends at school Carson will let her speak to, are also putting a lot of nasty stuff on social media and messenger. They are also being positively intrusive and bullying with their questions about what happened. She is likely not going to be calling anyone, but if she has that other phone, she can if she needs to."

"I see," Kelly said, picking up on the unspoken possibilities. "Do you think she is in danger?"

"Not just now, but once Carson knows you are interested in him, I can't predict. At the moment, he's anticipating Abbie being declared heir to the Hartley fortune and himself being a nominee for her. Tyrell hasn't told him yet that he won't be."

"I will advise the relevant people of your concerns," Kelly promised. "And I will ask about the phone. If I get the okay to return it, can you arrange it?"

David grinned. "There will be a way."

Kelly spoke his goodbyes to Kelso and headed out.

When they were alone, David glanced through the other reports Kelly had delivered. Kelso noted, "They matched the clothes you found to the man who attacked your wife, and obtained some excellent prints from the gloves."

"Don't those gloves have powder stuff in them?"

"Yes, to help get on, but if the hands sweat a lot..."

"Okay! Have you matched them?"

"They are being run through the computer, and will be sent interstate too."

"Have you any of Carson's prints?"

"Nothing obtained legally," Kelso specified.

"But?"

"Unofficially..." Kelso merely nodded once. "So your time line is going to be very important in deciding whether we have enough evidence to pick him up. So go have a power nap. I will wake you at ten, and you can finish adding the newest details to it."

"Right, I'll do that."

If he had thought the previous night's inquisition was intense, the 'briefing' that afternoon was gruelling. Not only were the official police investigators there, but the people who would decide if there was enough evidence to charge Carson with complicity in his daughter's abduction.

All the data from the various related investigations provided an impressive whole, even when unrelated possible irregularities were omitted.

David gave his overview of events, and fielded the questions asked to confirm the data he used. He referred to various reports by their filing number, and when asked, read the original information. Then the investigators checked details from interrogations of the men arrested for helping Delaney. Those men were not so tight lipped and while Delaney refused to talk, the others told what he had said to them.

David breathed more easily when the warrant was confirmed. The attack on Wanda hadn't been mentioned, but once Carson was processed, his prints could be cross referenced.

Kelso gave him an approving thump on the back, congratulating him as he packed up the equipment he had used during the session. "You will be having to teach your technique to us, I think."

"It helps that I was involved in the events to some degree, but it relies on everyone keeping accurate time records. When will they serve that warrant?"

"I think Des has been delegated with the task. He has organised to meet Carson later today and check him for scratches."

"He will have covered them," David predicted.

"Maybe not well enough," Kelso countered.

Carson answered the unexpected call with some satisfaction. The caller was a referral from another of his new recent clients. The man had arranged for them to meet in a private area of a swank hotel. That suggested that the potential client was well off.

He was dressed ready to leave, but was waiting for his daughter to get home. He had a surprise for her, aimed at keeping her docile and distracted.

Abbie trotted in, right on time and Carson called her over. "I have something for you."

"You do? What is it?"

"Just a minute."

Carson moved into his office and soon reappeared with a cardboard box. He placed it on the hall table, and let her look inside.

"Oh, Daddy! It's so cute! Is it a girl or a boy?"

She lifted out the tawny palm sized kitten and used a finger to stroke it.

"It's a girl. I was told. It must be for the damn thing scratched me. Seems to like you well enough though."

"What do I need to feed it?"

"I gave Mrs Buttrose the instructions I was given, and bought some kitten food. What will you call it?"

"I don't know," Abbie said. "I will have to think on it."

"Well, keep it in the box for now. We will need to house train it when we get some kitty litter."

Listening to the drivel his daughter was murmuring to the animal, made Carson smile. If the scratches were noticed, he had a logical cause.

The Maître d' escorted him to a private booth and provided a menu for drinks. Carson mentally ran over his sales speech and waited for his client to show up. It was a shock when someone else he knew came and took the other chair.

"Des, this is a surprise. I was expecting a client."

"I think you should ring your client and cancel," Des Kingley advised in a quiet voice.

Carson, quickly glanced around. He caught sight of two hovering, suited men that exuded the air of detectives.

"What is this about?"

"I have to ask you to come to police headquarters," Kingley said formally.

"Am I being charged with something?" Carson forced his posture to stay relaxed, even as Kingley was scrutinising his face.

"That will depend on your answers to certain questions. So, you should ring your client and cancel."

Carson decided that apparent compliance was the best idea, and made the call. He was unnerved enough to find the sudden ringing of a nearby mobile to be unrelated. The phone stopped ringing as his own was answered. He apologised to the man he spoke to, gave a plausible excuse, and promised to be in touch in the morning.

When he would have replaced the phone in his pocket, Kingley reached out and took it. One of the observing detectives came over and bagged it.

"What is this?" Carson demanded.

"We will talk in town," Kingley told him, standing up and gesturing for Carson to follow.

Carson had no choice, with the sharp eyes of the two detectives in him.

David wasn't invited to be present for the interrogation of Carson, but he knew, as a foreign consultant, it wasn't his business. Kelso, however, was with the Assistant Commissioner, observing from an adjacent room. He sent a text confirming when Carson had been picked up, and suggested he liaise with the police from Bellfield Station to keep an eye on Carson's wife, daughter and household. Carson's family had not been told of his – well he hadn't been officially arrested but he was as good as.

Once again, David agreed to watch Carson's house. There had been no overt activity since he'd heard of Carson's arrival in town. He wondered how his wife and daughter would react to his arrest. It wasn't his business, but he was concerned about a few possibilities.

If the warrant wasn't executed, or Carson made bail, he could do a flit – with or without the two women. Or he could tell his wife to leave – with or without Abbie, but more likely with. His wife might even decide to take off in her own account, since she had moved a large sum of Carson's money to her own name. Some of which had been moved further, without trace.

Unfortunately, the investigation of Carson's prior life was not advanced enough to provide a precedent for him being a flight risk.

David sat up straighter when the police car pulled up in front of him. When Kelly got out, he wound own his window to ask, "What's up?"

Kelly smiled grimly. "He has been charged with complicity in the abduction. I have been told to advise his wife, and I have Abbie's phone. It was deemed prudent to return it. We can't be certain that Carson won't get bail even though it will he set really high. If Carson flees, the girl will have the chance to decide to leave him."

"I hope it won't come to that," David said by way of thanks.

"So do I," Kelly agreed. "Do you want to come in with me?"

"Will we have a chance to go in?"

"I will suggest talking inside."

"I am not sure how his wife will take the news," David said with all seriousness. "If she faints or something, I can act as a paramedic."

Kelly smiled faintly, and seemed to accept the reason. David guessed he knew of the bug that was still transmitting from inside. It was time to retrieve it.

"I will let you slip the phone to the girl, will I?" Kelly suggested.

"If you like," David agreed, neutrally.

Keeping quiet as Kelly did his official task, David was observing reactions. He decided that Abbie wasn't as shocked as she should have been. She did stop petting the little creature in her hand and stared at them, taking in every word.

Kelly suggested they help Victoria Carson to a seat, and the housekeeper was quick to act. Abbie didn't follow, she was looking at him, not her mother.

"Was he involved," she asked bluntly, as soon as the others were in a small side room.

"Yes," David admitted tersely.

"Can you prove it?"

"The police have a very strong case." David chose not to admit his part in building the case.

Abbie seemed to be thinking.

"Do you want to hold Tinker?"

David was startled by the sudden suggestion, but decided to play along. He lifted the creature and asked, "How old is she?"

"Mrs Buttrose thinks only six weeks, and hardly old enough to leave its mother. Daddy gave her to me before he left, but he said she didn't like him because she scratched him."

"Did you see the scratches?"

"He had a scarf thing around his neck this morning, but I

didn't see anything when I got home," Abbie said as if it was of no matter.

David wasn't so sure.

"She wriggles a lot," Abbie said, her attention on the kitten. "Dad said to keep her in the box, but I put her down on the floor so she could explore. She made a beeline for under the chair."

"She is probably not used to the open space," David suggested, wondering what the girl was up to. She was gesturing him nearer a particular chair.

"Put her down. See if she does it again."

David obeyed, placing the kitten gently on the floor. She did indeed run under the chair.

"It will take her time to get used to this place," Abbie shrugged, "Can I get you to get her out."

Without commenting, David obeyed. He swept his hand gently under the chair until he felt tiny claws dig into his hand, and his fingers hit a small hard object. He swept it out as he carried the kitten.

Abbie pounced on Tinker, and began talking to her. David picked up the object and identified it as a small digital voice recorder.

Kelly emerged from the small room, leaving Victoria being fussed over by the housekeeper.

"What's this?" David asked, knowing Abbie had meant him to find it.

"I haven't seen it before," Abbie claimed. Then, with seeming innocence, went on, "When Daddy came in last night, he must have been carrying a box of stuff. I heard something drop and went to check. He was picking stuff back up and putting it in the box."

"What time would that have been?" Kelly asked casually.

"Oh, about eleven or quarter to, I think he had been home a while because he had changed into track pants and a hoodie."

"What did you do then?" Kelly asked.

"He told me to go back to bed and I did."

David quickly changed the subject. "I meant to give you this." He handed her the phone.

"Oh! Thank you," Abbie said quietly, slipping it out of sight into her pocket.

"It has been recharged," David went on. "You can call me if you need to, okay?"

"What about Wanda?"

"Her number will divert to mine for a bit."

"Is she in prison?"

"No. She had an operation. She was injured by a bullet when she tried to stop Delany taking you."

Abbie paled. "Did something else happen?"

Kelly nodded at David, tacitly giving permission to mention the incident.

"She was attacked at the hospital. She is just hanging in there."

"Will she be okay?"

"I know she is a stubborn bitch and doesn't intend to die till extreme old age," David said. "You don't need to worry about her." He looked at Abbie until she met his gaze. "It was not your fault, okay?"

Abbie nodded, her face pale again. David hoped she had comprehended his warning. She had given them a vital clue about her father, and should he find out, the girl was in for real trouble.

After a moment, she said, "Daddy won't let me go out much. He doesn't want anyone else to try for me."

"Have you ever had self-defence lessons?" David asked. She shook her head.

"Maybe you should," Kelly advised. "Goodnight, Miss Carson. You might like to go and help your mother. We will see ourselves out."

In the few moments before leaving, David quickly removed the device he had stuck under the edge of the hall table. Then, he looked around to decide what to do about the digital voice recorder. He pretended to examine it and 'accidently' set it playing. The computer voice, sounded very natural, as it spoke the words David recalled from one of the 'ransom' messages.

Kelly grew intent. "What have you there?" He hoped David's bug was still sending.

"This was under the chair where the kitten went."

"I think I will confiscate that," Kelly said formally. He took out a plastic bag to put it in.

David grinned, and they went back out to their cars.

"I don't know what will happen if the news gets out about Carson," David remarked.

"I hope it does," Kelly admitted. "If he has been scamming people like you think, it may bring more people to report him."

"If they want to admit they were scammed," David countered. "Is his current business being investigated?"

Kelly merely nodded. "What did Mainwright tell you?"

"One thing he mentioned was that his father used to do something related to time share places. Helping people who wanted to sell their time share. I believe there is an old investigation that is being reopened."

"Yes. What else?"

"The name Jacob Hillier was mentioned. I also heard it in relation to things Wanda learnt from Delaney. Something about a horse racing win prediction program."

"Will you and your partner be around to see that investigation through?"

"Wanda will want to, but we could be recalled at any time.

We really should have gone when the task force disbanded."

"What concerned you about the news getting wind of Carson's actions?" Kelly asked.

"Only how Abbie's school will react. I hope they don't decide to kick her out."

"I'll try to watch out for that," Kelly promised. "When are you due to be relieved?"

"About now. That's Fred's car up a bit. I will see you later," David said.

He watched Kelly drive off as he sat in his car to ring the hospital. He was put through to Wanda.

"I have been given the all clear and feel back to normal," Wanda told him.

"Then they will let you out?"

"You had better hurry, or I will leave before you get here."

"Don't you dare! Do you want me to bring anything?"

"Fresh clothes, make up, and a huge take away meal."

"Coming up. Stay there?"

"Of course. I've missed you."

It was as well that the ward was a private one, because the reunion was just short of X-rated. David did his own evaluation of his wife as they kissed.

"Not sure I really need a disguise," Wanda told him, "but I will do it to keep everyone guessing. So, Carson was picked up?"

David nodded. "Only in relation to the abduction though."

"Hope they hold him."

"They will. Overnight at least. He will be processed on charges of complicity in the abduction. Bail will be huge if granted."

"I wonder if he will run off, or try to bluff it out." Wanda grabbed the bag with the promised fresh clothes and began to get dressed.

"We will have to wait and see."

"Has Tyrell heard?" Wanda asked.

"I arranged to see him in the morning," David told her. "If the media latch onto the matter, he will probably read about it."

"How is it going with proving his guilt for last night's events?"

"There are still a few weak links, but Kelso and the police are onto it. And Abbie, say innocently, gave us an important piece of information."

"Has he got a hint of it?"

"No, and it seems he is in cover up mode. Kingley couldn't see any scratches, but I suggested ways he could have covered them and Kingley will have someone check again."

"Will I be allowed active status again?"

"Let's discuss that with Kelso. It might depend on what needs to be done. You still need to let your head heal more."

"Fair enough," Wanda agreed. "I will spend part of the next few days sitting in Kelso's back yard, absorbing the sun's rays, the Earth's aura, and wishing ill on certain people."

David breathed a quiet sigh of relief. His wife would be careful. "So, how are you feeling, balance wise?"

"Good, and you don't need to tell me it's still delicate."

"Wouldn't dream of saying it," David grinned, suspecting she had picked up his thought. "All we need to do then, is to keep you away from ill-advised potential assassins. Are you up to giving the police a statement?"

"Yes. I might have been a little dopey at the time, but I recall the details – up to a point."

"When you called me?" David asked. He was used to hearing her in his head.

"About then," Wanda agreed. "Do you think he thinks I'm dead?"

"The official story is that you are in a coma, barely hanging in there."

"Okay then, will I be required at his hearing on the abduction business?"

“I don’t think so. The prosecutor has your statement, and knows you are okay and can be summoned.”

“So, will that preliminary hearing be tomorrow?”

David nodded. “I expect he will get bail, and I hope he has to dig deep into his secret bank accounts to manage it.”

Wanda was busy changing the look of her face, making herself look Asiatic. When she finished, even someone who knew her well would not recognise her.

During the trip back to Kelso’s place, David brought her up to date on all the latest developments.

“Have you had instructions to return yet?” Kelso asked, and was relieved when David shook his head.

“What about your youngsters?”

“My father is trying to turn them into little savages,” Wanda claimed. “They are happy to be with their younger aunts and uncles, and a few younger cousins.”

“Good. Fred brought in the bundle of letters Maude gave you last week. You might start going through them.”

“That’s a point,” Wanda agreed. “I will jot down notes of anything that might help you find her other love-friend.”

Kelso wasn’t finished. “I also have the files on the deaths of Maude’s brothers and parents. You could also check the news archives about them. The brother’s deaths were ruled natural or accidental. Run your suspicious eyes over all the medical stuff.”

“I usually dislike desk work, but for this I will make an exception. Some things I picked up from the effluvium in Delaney’s mind, started to give me nasty ideas.”

“There was virtually no evidence to point to foul play,” Kelso warned.

“Perhaps a new viewpoint will be the key,” Wanda proposed. “I would say, at the time, no one could propose a motive. Hind sight has produced a few.”

"Indeed," Kelso agreed. "Now, David. I want you to go over everything Robbo told you, then we will get young Thea to join us."

"Where is she at the moment?" Wanda asked.

"I arranged for her to talk to her brother. She probably got there just after you left. I hope he will let her tell us things until he can bring us his physical evidence."

"Okay. I also have the files on the shonky adoption agencies to go through," David reminded Kelso.

"Yes, that is another key aspect, but that can wait for a bit."

Waking up next his wife, gave David the feeling things were finally getting back to normal. They rarely showed their deep affection to each other in the presence of others, but now they were alone, they did.

When they finally dressed and emerged for breakfast, Kelso took one look at them and smiled.

"What do you have planned for the day?" David asked him. "Since you have both of us tied to a desk."

"Thea, when she wakes, has stuff to tell us," Kelso said. "You and I will debrief her."

Since it was what he expected, David nodded. He asked, "Is there anything more we can do to help young Martin get back to school?"

"That young lawyer you're paying for is a very clever thinker. The drug squad team were well within their rights to charge him, and I'm sure you'll agree that most drug dealers try to deny ownership when drugs are found on them."

"But they weren't," Wanda protested.

Kelso glanced her way and said, "You are aware that no charges have been laid relating to his part in the ransom drop?"

Wanda nodded.

"Anthony Chan has requested a lab comparison of the drugs found in the case and samples taken from other recent cases. I think the results will be very interesting. Give it another day or so."

"What about the investigation into my misadventure?" Wanda persisted.

Kelso chuckled at her understatement. "I am sure you want the person charged with more than 'causing a misadventure'."

She glared at him.

"There are just a few pieces of corroboration still needed."

"When will Carson be pulled in for that?"

"That is not up to me. But the evidence against him is getting tighter. David mentioned that young Abbie innocently described her father's attire late Wednesday night – "

"Not so innocent, I suspect," David inserted.

"The description matches that of the man Martin saw getting into a taxi, and the one the taxi driver gave for the fare he took from the hospital to near Riverpark."

"Abbie and Martin are minors, oh I know Martin is 'emancipated', but would Abbie be allowed to testify against her father? Would it be wise?"

"Do you think Carson would come back at her if she did?" Kelso asked, concerned.

"From what Dav told me of his tirade after the abduction…I am damn sure he would."

David nodded, agreeing. "Did you mention to the investigators what she said? I would say he was removing more stuff from the house. Potential evidence."

"Like that voice recorder?" Kelso suggested. "That might be a delicate legal point. Neither you nor Kelly had a warrant to search or remove stuff from there. However, we can get a statement from Abbie, CCTV in the local area and near those storage units is being checked. His car is quite distinctive."

"His place has a double garage. Does his wife have a car? I think Dav mentioned the housekeeper driving some small car."

"Mrs Carson doesn't have a licence, and the housekeeper was out that night. The car she drove was hers."

Wanda merely looked at him, as If she thought he was missing a point. "You call yourself a policeman?"

"I've retired! We have had no reason to check the garage, but I see your point. If the other car David saw was hers, she may not have been using it that night. Motor registration is being checked. Carson does not have another car registered in his current name, and his other potential aliases have also been checked.”

“And that of his wife? Daughter? The Mainwrights?” Wanda suggested.

Kelso shook his head, “I really think the old cliché is true – about setting a thief to catch one...”

“I want to check that Stillman unit,” David persisted.

“There is not enough evidence for a warrant,” Kelso told him.

“Not even when Carson’s business phone has the same number as the person who called the unit manager? Carson strikes me as acquisitive, and reluctant to throw out useful information. If he hasn’t got all of his records on computer by now, and I’m guessing he doesn’t, that is likely where they are.”

“I am inclined to agree. The units are close... How do you think he will react if we reveal we are onto Stillman?”

“He’d grab what he could and run,” Wanda decided.

“Do you think he would destroy the rest?”

Wanda considered that carefully. “I think there would be a high likelihood. Stillman might be his last prepared identity. He would not want anything to tarnish it.”

“We do have several threads pointing to Stillman, and if our investigation into your attacker gives us more, it might be enough for a search warrant. The main problem is that what we might expect to find there won’t relate to the abduction or the attempt on your life.”

“Unless, we find evidence of his connection to Delaney,” Wanda proposed.

“I don’t think that will be very likely,” David had to say against the idea.

“Would it be enough to seal the unit until Stillman shows himself?” Wanda persisted.

“That may be an option,” Kelso considered.

“I think a check of the fire suppression system in those units would be advisable,” David suggested, and he sensed he’d out thought his wife. "Or even get a sniffer dog in."

That startled Kelso. "I'm getting old!"

Their conversation ended when Thea emerged, sleepy eyed, into the kitchen. They each moved to get their preferred breakfast. Then Thea spotted Wanda she went over and hugged her.

"I'm so glad you are okay. I heard what happened, and told Robbo how lucky he was."

"Well, the guy picked the wrong patient, as I don't intend to die until a really old age. Did Robbo say it's okay to talk to us?"

"Yeah. He heard how you saved his life. He said it changed his view of police types."

Wanda grinned. "Dav and I aren't police, and I have a really murky past."

Kelso murmured, "Help yourself to breakfast. We can talk after that."

"Fred told me that Carson was picked up," Thea blurted.

"Yes," Kelso confirmed. He considered how much to tell her. "He was charged with complicity relating to his daughter's abduction. A number of charges. Likely he will be able to pay the bail, but not until Saturday."

"He'll run, I reckon," Thea predicted.

"The option is that he will bluff it out, claim he did what he did to protect Abbie and Delaney took advantage. He is still thinking he can get at Abbie's real inheritance."

"Abbie's?"

"Yes, He has had her all these years, as the last Hartley heir."

"You are not going to let him do that to her?" Thea blurted.

David shook his head. "We've given the Hartley Trustees a head's up. They won't be having him as a signatory on any account they make for Abbie — even if the DNA test proves Abbie is Maude's daughter and he is her father. He doesn't suspect any of that, and thinks he's too clever to be caught."

"He had a go at me because I can testify that he knew Delaney, and we hope that information you and Robbo have can give clues to further evidence."

Any qualms Abbie still had were gone. The man she had always known as her father, and who her mother claimed loved her, was an out and out liar. If he loved her, it was as an object – the key to lots and lots of money. What's more, he considered her stupid. Did he think she was no better than the poor 'mad' woman who was supposed to be her real mother? And just because he had told her to do whatever he told her, and she'd had no option but to agree, he seemed to think that she had to take whatever he said as the absolute truth.

Well, she wasn't stupid. She had read news reports, and heard odd things from people.

She'd not said a word about having been found two full days before going home, and had made a vow to keep it that way. That David guy's mention of 'trying to catch the rest of the people in on the abduction' now seemed proof that the police had suspected her father.

Thinking of David, gave her reason to fantasize, just a little. Annie had said he was married, to Wanda. The pair being soul mates. That Wanda had turned up at the park that day suggested she had wanted to get to know her. Even realising that meeting had been contrived, did not make her angry. That she had provided uncritical protection during the second absolutely stupid period of her life, eclipsed it. She had probably been checking out her father, even back then. Now, her father was claiming she was involved in her abduction, and was demanding she be punished. He was a lousy hypocrite.

That morning, the second day of her community service had not been the same. Wanda had talked to her as an equal, an adult. It had been a new experience. She wished she could have been there again.

Instead, Annie had turned up. An absolute surprise. More so when Abbie realised Annie was as hopeless at gardening as she had been. She had been happy to help, and not at all annoyed at being told what to do. She was such a contrast to Gail.

"Have you heard anything from Wanda?" Abbie had asked, after they'd been working a while.

"Not directly," Annie admitted.

"David came and told us that my dad had been arrested. While he was there he said someone had attacked her and she was just hanging on..."

"Your father was arrested?" Annie blurted. "What for?"

"They reckon he was involved in my abduction."

"Was he?"

"I don't know. The police had him in town all afternoon, and Detective Kelly and David came to tell us. They haven't let him come home yet."

Abbie wasn't going to mention the voice recorder with the message about the ransom. It hadn't been her father's voice, but it had been suspicious. Just like his behaviour the previous night had been."

"I know something happened to Wanda. Martin had been at the hospital, visiting her after her operation. He saw the bloke, posing as a nurse, and again later when he had changed into dark pants and a baggy light coloured jumper. He saw him get a taxi."

"What did the guy look like?" Abbie asked, and she listened. The idea that it had been her dad put her stomach in a spasm.

"Tall, blond, had glasses," Annie summarised. "He had brown eyes, too."

Half those points fit her dad, as did the clothes.

"Wanda scratched him," Annie went on, as she took the hoe from Abbie to change tasks. "I would have been petrified, but I don't think Wanda was – even if they did have to resuscitate her."

"David said not to worry about her."

"Yeah, he told Martin that too. Do you think they are saying she's real bad, to lull the guy?"

Abbie decided they were. "She's tough, you know. Kelly suggested that I should learn self-defence."

"Wanda suggested that idea to Martin. Asked if he thought the school would let us learn for PE. He said, she said, she'd like to teach Mr Gill a lesson."

Abbie laughed, picturing the confrontation. "I don't think he'd be game to take her up on it. It would be beneath his dignity. I think she could probably take him on, even with one arm in a sling."

"I wouldn't disbelieve it," Annie said. "But I agree, you should learn."

"Because I keep haring off into trouble?"

"If you want to put it that way. I think that is why Wanda learnt."

"If the school won't do it, do you think you can learn outside?"

"Probably. I did."

"Oh, yeah, were you using that when Gail sent me to annoy you?"

"A bit," Annie admitted. "And when we were having our fight."

"Could you take out a bloke as big as my dad?"

"I haven't tried, but if a big guy grabbed me, I reckon I could get free,"

"When did you learn?"

"A couple of years ago, when my dad was working in Brisbane. Where we lived, wasn't the best area."

"I hope we can do it at school," Abbie said. "I don't think I will be allowed to do it otherwise."

Annie seemed about to say something, as Abbie leant over to pick up the dug up weeds. They'd touched briefly, and Annie had shut her mouth.

They worked in silence for a while, until the question in

Abbie's mind would no longer stay there. She had been puzzling over it since the start of term.

"How do you do that stuff when you touch things?"

"I don't know. It just started happening, and has been getting really horrible. My parents think I'm imagining things, so I can't really talk about it to them. I wanted someone who could help me, and I met Wanda just after that. She seemed to know what was happening, believed what I was saying, like she could look inside my head."

"I wouldn't like that," Abbie shivered. She was more imagining how horrid it would be if her father could.

"Can she do what you do?"

"She said not. She told me that sometimes she just 'knows things'. But she suggested some things that seem to help."

Annie decided to trust Abbie with more of her secret. She mentioned the 'mind trick' Wanda had taught her.

"I wish that would work on rotten memories."

"Maybe she could suggest something. I overheard David say that she doesn't forget anything."

"That doesn't sound promising."

"Well, maybe she has found a way to forget some things."

When Victoria Carson, newly resplendent from the beauty parlour, used a taxi to pick Abbie up, Abbie immediately felt the return of the oppressive depression.

Her mother started back on her maunderings – how she simply couldn't believe the bad things the police claimed about her Jeremy. She was still obsessing about, "what if he went to jail?"

"Mum! We'd be okay. You transferred a lot of his money, didn't you? We can live on that."

"But the house! It costs so much."

"We can get a cheaper place, that's just as nice but not so big," Abbie told her. "And didn't you transfer a lot of his money to yet another account?"

"Don't tell your father that. He won't like it."

"It was just a precaution, right," Abbie suggested. That wasn't quite how she'd understood the cryptic conversation she had overheard.

"I'll tell him that if I have to," Victoria said. Abbie merely shrugged.

"Have you heard anything from Daddy?"

"No, and I don't know why they are keeping him there."

"They will have to let you talk to him eventually."

"Yes, they will," Victoria cheered up immediately. "Jeremy will know what to do."

Abbie slipped upstairs as soon as she got home, wanting a shower to clean off all the dirt and sweat. It wasn't until she had stopped the water, that she heard the loud voices coming up from the lower level. From that, she could tell that her father was home, and in a really foul temper.

"Not going down there," Abbie murmured to herself, as she hurried to dry herself. She would do her hair in her room, with earbuds in and listening to her music.

That had been her intention, until she heard what her father was yelling. He was going off at her mother – about the money she had transferred on.

Her mother's voice wasn't steady as she said, "I did it just in case."

When her father abruptly moderated his tone, she was surprised.

"Maybe you did a smart thing, Victoria."

"Jeremy, how could they think you would ever harm Abbie?" Her mother's voice came clearly, more steady, but still upset.

"Probably that damn Delaney character," Carson claimed. "I don't even know how he got involved. All I did was ask an acquaintance to do me a favour and bring Abbie home. Those two con artists who have it in with me, could have used her as a hostage. I didn't want her hurt and I reckon that woman who came here one night, was in it with them. She probably got Delaney involved. He probably wants some of our girl's legacy since he was her step father for a few months."

Abbie had heard enough. She slipped quietly into her room, quickly brushed her hair and tied it back, then set out her homework, and put her music on. She had no intention of going down until she was sure her father had calmed down, or she was called for lunch. That summons came soon, with Mrs Buttrose knocking on the door.

"Lunch is ready, Miss Abbie, and your father is home."

Still not sure whether the housekeeper was meant to report on her, she decided to act surprised. "He is? Oh! I will be right down."

Her Dad was sitting at the table, and Abbie went over and gave him a hug. He was tense, but she felt him force himself to relax.

"I'm glad you are home," she lied.

"I'm back, Abbie. You don't have to worry."

"But they said —"

"I know. But I didn't do anything intending to hurt you. I just wanted you to be safe. You do know that."

Abbie just nodded, not trusting herself to speak in case she blurted out what she really thought.

"Go sit down so we can eat." Carson gave her a gentle nudge to move away.

Abbie has happy to get away from the big fat liar. If he had really wanted her safe, he would have told the police where he thought she was. He had to have told the other guy. If he had, Robbo would not have been badly injured, Wanda too. She would bet her father wasn't sorry either were hurt. She kept her eyes on her food until she finished eating the savoury pancakes Mrs Buttrose had made.

Back in her room, she found Tinker was awake and trying to reach the top edge of the box. She lifted the tiny creature onto the desk and gave her a finger spinner to play with.

Her phone rang. The one her father had bought.

"Hi Abs. How come the Charity Case was working with you? What did she do?"

"Nothing," Abbie told her friend.

"Aw, come on, Abs! The only people who would do that are people who have to."

"Gail, a lot of those there are volunteers. They call themselves 'Friends of Riverside Park'."

"Sure, Abs," Gail dripped sarcasm, implying she knew better. "I bet she pinched something. After all, she doesn't have all the advantages we have."

"She did no such thing!"

"You've gone soft in the head, Abs. She's trying to muscle in on us. Has been since the start of term."

"So? Why's that a problem?"

"I don't like her," Gail stated.

"She ignores us at school," Abbie said, hoping to end the conversation.

"I thought you said your Dad wouldn't let you talk to just anyone?"

"He wasn't around."

"Tell me all, on Monday," Gail directed, then hung up.

The call left Abbie feeling worse. What would Gail say if she learnt her father had been arrested? Worse, what if she ever found out she had given the police evidence against her father? Actually, she hadn't given it to the police. David had found it. Yeah. She had never seen it before...before the previous hour.

Tinker tired of the game with the finger spinner and began pushing her head under Abbie's hand and meowing. Deciding the kitten was probably hungry, Abbie took her down to the kitchen, and asked Mrs Buttrose for some milk.

"Don't give her too much. She will have her dinner just before yours."

"I won't," Abbie promised. She watched as the housekeeper poured a little milk into a glass, and went to the pantry to get some of the pellet like kitten food. This she put in a small plastic container.

"Let the dry food soak before you give them to her."

"Okay."

Before she left, she dared to ask, "Where's my Dad?"

"In his office. I wouldn't bother him. He and your Mum are talking."

Abbie shrugged, but the feeling of lead in her stomach had returned. She hurried back upstairs, determined to bury herself in homework. That, at least, was something she could control and she had a lot to catch up on.

Sunday, by contrast, was so quiet that Abbie felt she needed to tip-toe around the house. Her father stayed in his office, with the door firmly shut. Her mother barely emerged from her bedroom. She didn't dare ask what was going on.

Monday, when her father was at the breakfast table as normal, reading the paper, dressed for work – Abbie began to relax. She hoped he'd leave the paper, but he never did. He seemed relaxed, perhaps because his 'mistaken' arrest hadn't made the headlines and he wouldn't have frightened off his clients. He left before Abbie needed to, and she took the opportunity to test the door of his office. It was firmly locked.

Gail and Clare met her when she arrived. "Do you have money today?"

"No. I told you Daddy wasn't giving me any until after I finish community service."

"You'll owe us heaps when you do."

"Why? You're not buying anything for me."

"If you don't want anything, that's your look out. We had a deal!"

"We'll need to change it!" Abbie stated, expecting an outburst from Gail, but she was staring at something over her shoulder. She turned as Gail said, "What's Kemple doing here? I wonder if Gill knows."

Episode 26

Change of Luck

<u>Chapter 1</u>

On Sunday, when Kelly visited him and told him he was to be in court at 11, Martin felt himself go pale.

"Does my lawyer know?" was all he could think to say.

"He will have been advised. Didn't you receive notification yesterday?"

"No. How should it have come?"

"By text message."

Martin checked his phone. No messages.

"Go and get yourself dressed tidily. Do you have a tie?"

"Just the school one."

"Use it. Be quick. We have half an hour to get you to the Children's Court and give you time to talk to your lawyer."

"What's going to happen?"

"We can talk later."

Martin was perversely glad he'd had so little warning. He would have been sick with worry had he known.

"I thought my case wouldn't come up for ages."

"Your lawyer put in a good case to have it expedited. I'm sure you'll be glad to be able to be back at school."

"Only if Gill has his nose rubbed in my exoneration. Assuming the best."

"Do you have doubts?"

"Thousands of them. People keep accusing me of things, and even when nothing is proved, believe the accusations. So what is going to happen?"

"Well this is a special session," Kelly explained. "You will get to tell your story to a judge. There will be witnesses for and against you. The judge will decide if there is enough evidence to take the charges further. It will be held in a closed court because of its links to other cases."

Martin didn't know what to say.

"Are you alright?" Kelly asked.

"I'm scared," he admitted.

"There's no one you'd like to have in court with you? Someone who knows you well?"

Martin shook his head. "David, but he'd only known me a few weeks. If the bastard who sired me wasn't such a low-life...he's the one who should know me best. I definitely don't want him here. Heck, in terms of know me, you and your mates know me next best, but they are always asking me if I've done stuff."

"I could give you a character witness," Kelly offered.

"Dare I ask what that's likely to be?"

"My personal opinion. Not any department agreed version."

Martin tried to be unobtrusive when he wiped the moisture from his eyes. "Thanks. I really didn't know who I could ask."

Even after talking to his lawyer, Martin felt like he wanted to throw up. He was told to plead 'not guilty', although at some preliminary session, his lawyer had done that for him. He hardly dared look around as he followed his lawyer into the court. Kelly had said it was to be a closed court, but there seemed to be a lot of people in the seats.

A faint humming, that he somehow heard even with the formalities going on, was teasingly familiar. He was distracted for a moment as a voice seemed to say, "Stand straight. Look at the judge as you speak. You are innocent. Tell only the truth."

It hadn't been his lawyer, but he felt he should know the voice. The advice was good, and he shook himself slightly to ease the tenseness in his muscles.

When he was directed to sit, Martin caught a glimpse of the people directly behind him. His heart leapt. David was there. He didn't recognise the woman next to him, but the person winked at him. Mrs Sutton was there, and Mr Baxter. He felt torn between gratitude and wanting to hide. He didn't have a chance to look further.

Then there was no chance to think, the man acting as prosecutor was beginning to introduce the evidence against him. He wanted to listen, catch everything, so he could speak against it if he had to.

He wanted more and more to shrink into the hard chair. The drug squad officers had acted on information received, creditable information. Listening, trying to feel like an outsider, it sounded so bad.

The odd humming began again, easing his breathing, brushing some of his fear away. After a while, he recognised it. *Wanda!* In the cells at Kew. *She was here! She was alright!*

His lawyer began speaking against the charges, until the judge directed questions to him. The advice he felt sure had come from Wanda, buffered him. He answered candidly, honestly, and tried to decide how the judge was taking it. Her face betrayed nothing. When directed, he went back to his seat and tried to understand the scientific talk of a man his lawyer had invited in.

The faint thread of thought that wasn't his own, said, "All you need to know is the drugs in the case have been linked to other cases, that you could not possibly have been involved in. The faint traces on you, from sitting or lying where a faint layer of drug dust must have been, is not incriminating."

That was all he needed. It finally seemed he was headed for clear space.

His claims of events from when Delaney took him to when he was arrested, were confirmed when Kaspersky took the stand and gave a report. Yet it seemed that mention of Abbie being found in his garage had caused the judge to doubt him.

Then his lawyer called David, and as he walked past, he sensed David was very definitely in his official persona – like he had been that night in the park. His identification as part of the Atlas Task Force, drew immediate attention. He told the judge how Martin's actions had been forced upon him by Delaney, and he gave a detailed timeline of events that occurred during the Carson abduction. It seemed to have covered everything and settled all doubts. Then Chan, his lawyer, introduced character witnesses, and he felt himself blushing. Mrs Sutton told of how he had asked for somewhere at school to do his homework, because he couldn't at home. She was able to confirm that his work was at a satisfactory level.

Mr Baxter, told of how he had volunteered to help the scouts, had found the unpleasant remains under the house and had handled himself as a mature adult. David returned and told how he had been concerned for Maude Delaney, and helped her and defended her. Kelly, as promised, also spoke for him. He mentioned the many suspicions that had fallen on him, and the complete lack of evidence to suggest his complicity or involvement in any crimes.

Finally, the judge announced a brief recess and left via a door at the back of the judge's bench. The court usher directed participants to remain inside the room, but they could move around, but not past the lawyer's tables.

Martin wanted to approach the strange Asian looking woman with David. He was sure it was Wanda, but his eyes could scarcely believe it. He glanced that way, then asked his lawyer, "How does it look?"

"I believe, all went well."

"Why did the judge go out to think on things?"

"Possibly because one of the spectators is a very high ranking policeman, who hasn't shown which side of the case he is on."

Martin looked around and guessed who it was. "There are a couple of others that I don't know."

"One is from the Juvenile Justice Department. Another is from DHS. One reason I requested this special hearing was because your school was not letting you fulfil one of the bail conditions, and the conditions of your Youth allowance."

"I told Gill he had no right. He didn't seem to care," Martin said. "If it wasn't for Annie, I wouldn't even be getting worksheets and notes."

"Well, when the case against you is dismissed," Chan said encouragingly, "Your teacher will be able to attest to the fact, and perhaps take a letter to your school."

"I hope you are right," Martin murmured, then had a horrible thought, "They won't make me be fostered, will they?"

"Wait for the verdict. Then worry about that."

Martin practically floated out of the court, the heavy weight of fear and worry was gone. He thanked Chan, and received a nod of acceptance. He felt Baxter give him a slap on the back, and heard him repeat some of what he'd said earlier.

David was keeping his distance, acting serious, but the eyes of the Asian woman were dancing above a wide grin. The drug squad officers left quickly, as did Kaspersky. Kelly asked first if he needed a lift home. Martin shook his head, and murmured, "Thanks."

"You impressed me today, Martin," Mrs Sutton told him. "I have seen a whole new side of you. Why do you act so different at school?"

"You know why. You know what everyone thinks," Martin challenged her. "I know being called names and accused of things isn't a reason to punch everyone who does. They aren't worth arguing with. I let them think what they like, say what they will, so long as I can learn stuff."

"I see. You and your friend Annie have certainly opened my eyes lately."

"Will you confirm with Mr Gill that I can return tomorrow?"

"You should get a call or a text, but even if you don't, I want to see you in my class tomorrow."

Jeremy Carson felt his new phone vibrate and pulled into a side street to stop and answer it.

"Lonny? What is it?"

"Just heads up, mate. There's cops all over the place around here. Checking all the bins."

"So?"

"Well, it's just that the local garbos haven't been around like they should have. Some dispute they have on."

"What about the dumpsters?"

"Them too."

"Right. Thanks Lonny."

"Jeremy? What's up?" Victoria asked, sensing his worry.

"Change of plans. I need to get to the bank."

"What's happened?"

"Nothing I can't handle." He wasted no time re-joining the main road traffic.

Victoria waited in the car while he went into the bank. She had never been privy to everything Jeremy did, but now she knew more than she wanted. Her husband might go to jail, all because he had tried to keep Abbie out of danger. Oh, he said he wouldn't, but he'd had her boxing up most of the stuff in their bedroom all of yesterday. She had only left out a couple of changes of clothes. He said they might have to leave and go where no one knew them. But it wasn't supposed to be until after Abbie had been confirmed as the Hartley heir. She knew he intended to look after Abbie's inheritance. He would need to. Abbie had been showing precious little sense lately. It was still so unreal that she was the missing Hartley child. Jeremy had told her they only needed to wait for the DNA results — maybe another week.

His court appearance was still several months off. So far, at least, her friends and the people she talked to, hadn't heard about him being charged and she wasn't going to mention it. It was all going to blow over anyway.

Carson returned, but as far as Victoria was concerned, he was in a bubble of his own. She might as well have been on the moon. He drove off, not towards where they had planned to have lunch, but towards the city. It seemed his full concentration, apart from driving, was considering some problem.

At the Casino, he drove into the carpark and finally acknowledged his wife. "Stay here."

Victoria tried to object, but her husband had already locked the door and was striding towards the entrance. She was more than a little irritated. Something was wrong.

When he returned, he was smiling. "I have booked us on a week's holiday. A change of pace."

"Abbie too?"

"No. She can stay with Mrs Buttrose. I will tell her it is a test of how well she behaves. Besides, she says she has catching up to do at school. Do you want to see a movie?"

Victoria was instantly diverted. "Oh, yes!"

"They have a cinema here. Why don't you choose the picture, buy two tickets and text me the details?"

"I don't know your new number."

"Use the business one. I have all calls diverting to this one."

"But you said they kept the business one."

"It's no problem. They think I can't use it anymore. Just do as I say. I have a few things to do and then I will join you."

Victoria couldn't recall when she had last seen a movie, and decided not to worry about what her husband was up to.

Carson went to the café and waited for his contact to arrive.

Hal Johnson was someone he'd known all his life and could be trusted implicitly. They had both helped each other out of trouble a few times over the years. Johnson wasn't Hal's birth name, any more than Carson was his.

"You were right, J. They are onto you. What did you do?"

"Never mind! What did you hear?"

"Something about DNA."

"I had a test to prove I was the father of the child of a rich widow," Carson stated.

"No, not that, Did they take a sample while they had you?"

"Yes, but they said that was routine." Carson felt the scratches on his neck begin to prickle. No one could see them now. Lonny had done his magic and now there was a layer of fine plastiskin covering them. There was no way the police could link him to that bitch's death. He hoped she would die.

"Yeah, mate. They compare it to old crimes and I heard mention DNA from old hair."

"You must have heard wrong, Hal."

"What I heard was hair from twenty years ago."

Carson breathed a gutter curse he never normally expressed. How could the police have got hair from back then?

"It will take a while for any results to come back. Still, I think I will have to leave. Can you transfer a bank check to another account so the trail is muddied?"

"Can a duck swim?" Hal grinned. "So, who will you be when we meet next?"

"I will let you know. Meantime, can you organise a van and people to do a thorough end of lease clean of my place?"

"When?"

"Tomorrow. 9am. Not before. They have to be finished by three at the latest. They need to do everywhere, except my daughter's room. I will have her do in there."

"Usual rate?"

"Of course." Carson passed over an envelope of cash, and

another containing a bank cheque that almost cleaned out his current everyday account, as well as the details for the final account.

"Do that transfer fast, okay?"

"Are the cops that close? Haven't you learnt yet?"

"That damn Delaney...never mind. What else have you learned?"

"You mentioned Delaney. He's gone for sure for taking your daughter and killing that guard. I doubt he will get out of prison alive."

"The fool wanted his share of an investment, but he's ruined it. Maybe there is a work around, but it will mean leaving the payoff for a few more years."

"Why did you even use him?"

"Long story, but those two bastards of Dolly's managed to find me. I didn't want my girl in their clutches."

"Was one of them the one you tried to silence?" Hal made a stab in the dark, and grinned when Carson swore.

"How did you hear of that? I was disguised."

"Not well enough, or you left a trail a moron could follow. It sounds like they almost have enough to pull you in."

Carson didn't admit that he had felt the police breathing down his neck. "I'm leaving tomorrow. I have taken everything that matters out of the house, and when I go, it will be like I am just going to work. Get your people to put everything else in a storage place and send me the key. When that job's done, I will need someone to empty another unit. It's not in my name, and the police shouldn't know about it."

"J, you're definitely losing it. You should have got everything digitised, and destroyed the evidence. If you do flit, and the cops do have an inkling, they will seal it."

"I do have the important stuff on disc – mostly. Some of the stuff was too sensitive to let anyone else see it. Anyway, if the place should happen to be sealed, here's the solution."

Hal stared at the device Carson put in his hand. "You have some incendiary device in there?"

Carson smiled grimly. "I have survived this long, and kept ahead of the police. I don't intend to end my career in jail. This last investment should see me set for retirement."

He stood and said, "Let me know if you hear anything else, Hal."

Once away from the café, Carson checked his phone, found Victoria's text and headed to the cinema. The pretence of watching the film would give him time to consider his changeover plans.

"What are you doing here, Kemple?" Gail challenged as he was about to walk past.

"Here?" Martin pretended to be surprised. "Well, I'm enrolled here. Surprised you've never noticed." He went to walk on, but Gail wasn't finished.

"Does Mr Gill know?"

"I'm sure he does by now," Martin said cheerily.

"Why? Was it in the paper? Drug pusher freed to sell drugs to school kids?"

"Oh, don't get me confused with my cousins and their friends," Martin grinned. "If they try anything like that again, their step-dad will send them to their overseas relatives."

"Gerry has never..."

"Fortunately, they weren't caught like Tory and Jordan who are both still awaiting trial."

"Why aren't you?"

"Because the police were able to prove I was set-up."

This time Martin did keep walking off, and something about him made Gail snarl. "What's got into him?"

Abbie had wondered the same thing. He wasn't slouching and acting shifty. Maybe Annie would know. She'd ask her on the way to maths class.

Just then Clare and Helen trotted up and reminded them of the time.

Martin was cornered by Gill before he reached the lockers. The conversation caused him to arrive a little late for homeroom, but when he walked in, he was smirking. He caught Annie's glance his way and grinned, and moved to a seat fairly near her.

In the few minutes between homeroom and English, he

joined her, but spoke to Naomi. "Can you tell your Dad I really appreciated him speaking up for me yesterday?"

Surprised, Naomi said, "Sure. You seem happy today."

"Oh, I am. I had my day in court yesterday. Ms Sutton was also there. Mr Gill wasn't so pleased to see me back, but he can't say anything."

Karen added a quiet word. "Actually, he got an official letter. A copy of the one my aunt got for the school. There was a bit about the fact that the school was not letting you fulfil some of your bail conditions by letting you attend."

"So that's what had him in a knot," Martin smirked. "I told him he had no right to suspend me, and he as good as said, 'Who's going to complain.' I think he found out."

Annie had been dropped off at school by her dad that morning, and hadn't seen Martin until he came in.

"I didn't know you'd be in court yesterday."

"Neither did I until Kelly came to pick me up."

"Dad had a call just after breakfast," Naomi told him. "It must have been about that, because he rang one of the other scout leaders to say he'd be tied up all morning."

"If anyone asks me about you, I'll say you have been cleared of any wrongdoing," Annie told him.

"Actually, it might be fun to add that I am meant to tell the police of anyone who still claims I am guilty."

"Are you?" Naomi challenged.

"A friend suggested that it might make people think twice."

"I bet I know who that was," Annie grinned.

Martin winked and said, "David was there yesterday as well."

"Was that the guy with the American accent that was at the scout house?" Naomi asked.

"Yes," Annie confirmed. "He and Wanda seem to be excellent judges of character. I saw David put the wind up Martin's cousins."

Martin laughed. "For which they blame me. Anyway, see you later."

On the way to Maths, Abbie asked, "Hey, Dusty. What's with Kemple today?"

"He's glad to be back at school, and the charges he was facing were dropped. The judge felt he had been set up."

"Was all that related to me being found at his place?"

"No. They knew he couldn't have been involved in that."

"Oh! Isn't that David heading towards Admin?"

"It is!" Annie agreed. "Wonder what he's doing here?"

"Maybe it's about Martin," Abbie sniggered.

Annie laughed. "Or that self-defence idea."

"Why don't you ask him?"

"If it's our business, we'll find out," Annie decided, as they reached their classroom.

Annie had been right. They received a notice about it that afternoon. The offer was for students in years 10, 11 and 12, and would involve a cost. There would be four sessions, run during regular PE periods, and anyone who opted out would be doing the regular PE activities. The sessions would be starting early next term.

At the lockers, there was a lot of interest, and Annie wondered how David would manage dozens of students. That's if he was able to stay in Australia that long.

Later, as she was walking home, she quizzed Martin.

"Oh, I reckon he will arrange for others to help. It's probably why there is a cost."

"Almost everyone was interested," Annie said.

"Yeah, but if their parents have to pay, many may not. They still have to pay for the school camp later in the year."

"When's that?"

"Second term. You likely to go?"

"Will you be?"

"If I can save up enough, or my mother agrees to cover the cost."

"It should be fun. Where do they go?"

"Not sure about this year. The usual place had a fire go through last year. We will probably find out when they send the details home."

Annie got back to the previous topic. "I'm going to ask dad if I can do the lessons. I've done a bit before, but it was ages ago."

"I want to as well," Martin admitted, thinking he'd like to be able to tackle his father, or Mickey Delaney. "I think it will do Abbie good. I wonder if the Hell's Angels will come down to Earth and try it. If Wanda was teaching, I don't think she would take nonsense from them."

"I wonder how she really is," Annie mused.

"At my hearing, David had someone with him. I'm totally sure it was Wanda, but you wouldn't have known by just looking at her. She looked Asian."

"I know what you mean. Last week end, went I went to see Maude, I saw someone talking to Maude's trustee. I'm pretty sure it was her."

"I think Abbie's dad is just as good at changing his appearance," Martin said, surprising Annie.

"Whoa! Where does he come into it?"

"I saw the bloke who attacked Wanda. I'm pretty sure it was him."

"You're not going to accuse him?"

"Not to his face, and anyway, I don't have to. But the guy recognised me, and then kept his head turned away as he hurried off. I am pretty sure David is working to trace his movements."

"But why would he do such a thing?"

"Because Wanda can pin him down to a part in Abbie's abduction," Martin said soberly. "Anyway, they found the gloves the guy used and are hoping to get prints from them."

Annie shook her head. "I can't even imagine my father doing anything like that or even wanting the money Abbie might be entitled to."

"That's because your dad is nice and sensible. I won't mention mine, but Carson is just a greedy, covetous bastard. He deserves to go to jail."

"What will happen to Abbie if he did?"

"She's still got her mother. But I don't think we should mention our suspicions about her father. We could be wrong."

"I think she had some suspicions of her own," Annie said carefully.

"Did you get that from touching her stuff?"

"No, well maybe. She had a funny expression on her face when I mentioned the guy you saw at the hospital. She wanted to know what he looked like."

"All I can say is maybe we should keep an eye on her and help her if she needs it," Martin suggested. "Like you've helped me."

Abbie was in the middle of getting her books out for class when her phone vibrated. She glanced around, checking no teachers were close, before getting her phone out to check the message.

She was unaware that she had begun to scowl as she read it, until Annie nudged her and then she put the phone back in her pocket. She wasn't meant to have it on, or even on her, but it gave her a sense of security. She forced a more natural expression as she walked off with Helen and Clare.

Once she was out of the way, Martin squatted down to get his stuff. Annie was still at her locker and he gave her a quizzical look.

"All I got was she was annoyed," Annie admitted. "The touch wasn't long enough for anything else."

"What about, I wonder. She was happy enough before it."

"I heard her tell Gail that her parents would be having a week away for their anniversary. Maybe something else came up."

"Like her dad getting arrested again?" Martin murmured hopefully.

"No, like they weren't going to be going at all."

"Maybe, but this time the housekeeper lives in. So, probably she was hoping for him to be away a bit."

"We'd better hurry," Annie suggested.

They both moved off, not obviously together, but they both had science next.

During science, Annie kept an eye on Abbie, but she seemed back to normal.

It wasn't until they were getting ready to go home, that Annie got an inkling of something out of the ordinary. Abbie shoved past Gail to get to her locker, ignoring her friend's acidic comments and began shoving things into her school bag. In her haste, she dropped her science prac book and Annie lifted it up for her.

"Don't get any ideas, Charity Case!"

"Ideas? Like you're in a tearing hurry?" Annie retorted. "I already figured that out."

"Yeah, my dad's picking me up and he won't like having to wait."

Martin commented without looking at Abbie. "Won't be your fault if you get there so quickly he has to wait for the other parents to get out of his way."

Abbie didn't acknowledge that she had heard, but she did slow down.

Martin finished at the lockers and wandered off as he usually did. This time, he didn't go far, and he took out his phone to call someone. When Annie started to head to the back gate, he whistled and waited for her to turn before shrugging towards the front of the school. They joined the general exodus, with Martin in the lead, and Annie realised he was following Abbie. He stopped where he had a good view of the carpark. Annie caught up.

"See if you can spot Carson's silver Mercedes," Martin whispered to her. "Or whatever car she gets into. I'll explain later."

Annie moved closer to Abbie, who was within a crowd of other students that was gradually thinning out as parents picked up and drove off. She edged back to where Martin was before it became obvious she was watching Abbie. No silver Mercedes drove in, and when the two school busses had left, only a handful of students remained waiting for pick up. Martin pulled her back towards the admin block before he made another call. "It's Martin. She's still here, waiting."

"I think she's calling someone," Annie said quietly. Martin nodded and glanced at her to let her know he's heard. "What should we do? What if something has happened to her parents?"

Martin covered the microphone of his phone. "David is checking something."

Annie looked back towards Abbie, just as her phone rang. "It's Abbie," she said quickly, before answering.

She put the call on speaker so Martin could hear.

"Hi Abbie."

When they heard the note of panic in Abbie's voice, Martin whispered, "Tell her we will come back. We haven't gone far."

As Annie did that, Martin moved away and spoke into his phone. His expression became a scowl, and all he said was, "Okay, we will see you there."

He gestured for Annie to trot back towards the back gate. She took a quick look at Abbie, who was walking slowly, still watching the carpark for a sign of her father.

"He's not likely coming," Martin said, slowing behind the music rooms. "David told me he was followed to the casino in town, and his car is still in the carpark."

"How long ago did he go there?" Annie asked.

"David didn't say, but he wants us to stay with Abbie. We can tell her I was held up talking to Ivan. We can suggest walking home with her. David will meet us there."

They waited a few minutes longer then head back towards where they last saw Abbie. She saw them and ran over.

"Daddy was meant to pick me up."

"Does he know what time we get out?" Martin asked.

"Oh! I don't know. Mrs Buttrose has been picking me up. She told me he would so..." Abbie trailed off. Then she said, "But it's odd. I thought I had figured out the reason he was picking me up."

"What was that?" Annie asked.

"Well, Daddy said he was taking Mum away for a week, for their anniversary. The only thing I can think off that would make him change plans would be if heard from Mr Tyrell and he asked to see us."

Martin didn't let on he knew what she was talking about.

Annie said, "That's possible. Did you try ringing him?"

"Yes. Him, Mum, Mrs Buttrose – none of them are answering. I don't know what to do. I still have a bus ticket, but the busses have gone."

"Let me ring someone," Martin suggested as he began dialling David's number. For Abbie's benefit, he apologised to David for ringing and then asked if he could check on Mrs Buttrose, who should have come if the Carson's were held up. David had agreed, and rung off quickly, but Martin pretended to listen, gave an 'okay' and hung up.

"I rang David. He said he'd met you."

Abbie perked up.

"He suggested we walk home with you, but you should keep trying your parents and housekeeper. Likely your parents were held up and will call you when they are on their way. You can tell them where you are."

"Annie, will your parents worry if you're late?"

"They won't be home yet, but I will text them and let them know I will be late. If mum gets home before me, she will check her messages."

Martin led the way, going out through the back. He stayed ahead, in case Abbie wanted to talk to Annie.

When they reached her house, Abbie rushed up to the door, dragging her keys from her pocket. She tried to fit the key in the lock. "What's wrong? It won't go in."

"Here, let me try," Martin offered. Abbie handed the keys over, her hand was shaking.

He tried, and discovered Abbie was right. He then looked at the lock and her keys. "Are you sure this is the right key?"

"Of course!" Abbie retorted, sounding a bit more like her normal self.

"Well, these are for a Whitco lock, and the lock is Lockwood."

Abbie shoved him aside to look for herself. Then she collapsed onto the step. Annie sat down beside her and gave her a hug, picking up what she didn't want to say.

"What did I do to deserve this," Abbie said, beginning to sob.

Martin spoke up, sharply, intensely. "Nothing! You did nothing. The person to blame is your father."

"What do you mean?"

"I reckon he has done a runner."

"What about my mother?"

"I don't know," Martin admitted, not liking some ideas that came to him. "Look Abbie, I don't want to get you mad at me, but I overheard a few things I probably wasn't meant to. I think the police were about to arrest him again, on other charges, and he got wind of it."

Abbie, still shaking, didn't respond.

"Abbie?" Annie prompted.

"He's despicable!" Abbie blurted. She turned to Martin. "Annie told me that you saw the person who tried to kill Wanda. Was it him?"

"It didn't look like him," Martin had to admit.

"Was he wearing..." Abbie described what she had seem her father in late Thursday night.

Martin nodded, he hadn't told Annie it was a hoodie the guy had on, but Abbie had seen that much. She told them, "That's what I saw my dad wearing. He never wears stuff like that. I don't want to be here when he comes back."

"David is on his way. He will know what to do," Martin said.

Kelly squatted down in front of Abbie and asked, "Do you know what your parents intended to do today?"

Kaspersky went over to the stranger and was asking questions. From his initial answers, Martin guessed he represented the firm that rented the house. Martin was trying to listen to that conversation, as well as listening to Abbie's answers. He was also aware of the Asian woman who was examining the lock of the door. She winked at him, before slipping away and disappearing around the side of the house.

Hoping that Annie was concentrating on the conversation between Kelly and Abbie, Martin moved over to David and asked, "Found him?" His answer was a head shake, "There is a warrant out for him."

"He must have got wind of it," Martin suggested.

David gave a terse, "Yes," before becoming intent on what the agent was saying.

"He called us at two-thirty to say he had vacated. I'd just got back to the office after bringing the locksmith."

Kaspersky asked, "Do you have the new keys?"

"No, Sir. I'd handed them in. I can send for them."

"Do that please."

"What's going on?" the man asked, not moving.

Kaspersky didn't answer. Instead he asked, "Did you go in?"

"Yes, but only on the ground floor. We checked a few rooms and all seemed in order. We will have a thorough inspection done tomorrow."

"Did you get a forwarding address?"

"No. Mr Carson hadn't arranged accommodation yet. He promised to do so once settlement on a particular property was made. He only said that was in Port Macquarie."

"We will need a statement from you, Mr Lewis," Kaspersky advised. "Now, if you would, can you arrange for the keys?"

Lewis headed towards his car, and Kelly, aware of what the agent had said, asked Abbie, "Did your father mention anything about moving?"

"No, and where's all my stuff?"

Kaspersky said, "We'll take a look around inside."

Abbie made to stand up and was told, "You young people need to wait outside until we have checked."

Annie's phone rang and she spoke to her mother. "I'm at Abbie's place. Something odd is going on." She listened, then explained, "No, she's fine, but no one came to pick her up from school...I'll let you know, Mum, but I'm okay. Martin is here, and Detective Kelly and David. But Mum, if Abbie needs somewhere to sleep tonight, can I bring her home? Thank's, Mum, I'll tell her."

Abbie burst into tears, but managed a strangled, "Thank you."

Wanda returned and spoke quietly to Kelly. Abbie didn't notice her until Kaspersky asked, "Should you be here?"

Undaunted, the reply was, "The overwhelming consensus was no, but I am willing to tempt fate in this instance."

Abbie twisted around, and moved to give her a hug.

"I'm fine, Abbie," Wanda assured the girl, while returning the hug.

"Did my Dad try to kill you?"

Even though she was sure, Wanda only said, "I was a bit out of it, and it didn't look like him. The police are investigating."

"Martin said the person was tall. It could have been him. What if he tries again?"

"Let him," Wanda said grimly. "The person who attacked me won't have any advantages next time, and I was taught a lot of dirty tricks from a marine drill sergeant.”

“Are you going to be at school to teach us?”

“I get the idea you want to see if I am just bragging,” Wanda teased. “Yes, I’d like to be, but whether I actually do more than supervise, is up to my minders. Give me a week, and I’ll be back to being dangerous.”

Abbie, wiped her eyes and drew a deep breath. She watched the agent talking to someone in a car and then bringing a bunch of keys up the path. He made a production of unlocking the door. Abbie, tried to go in, but Wanda held her back.

“Wait, here, okay? We will have a look first – just to be careful.”

With Lewis protesting that everything was in order, Wanda followed the two detectives inside.

Annie distracted David by asking, “Could she really take on Abbie’s dad? She’s not much taller than we are and I don’t think I could.”

“That would depend on your motivation, and how much practice you do to build muscle and maintain it,” David told the three students. “None of you really need to be that good. Being able to get free and run away is your best option.”

Martin suggested then, “Why don’t you try calling your Mum again, Abbie.”

Kaspersky returned to the door and beckoned the three students in. Lewis was explaining, “The furniture came with the house. I have a full list of everything.”

“My bed didn’t,” Abbie said belligerently.

“Miss, I think I know what did and didn’t,” Lewis told her.

“I live here,” Abbie replied.

“Not any more!”

Kelly inserted himself into the conversation before it became an argument. “Abbie, we need you to look around carefully, and tell me if anything looks odd. Detective Kaspersky will go with you.”

Once they'd moved off towards the kitchen area, Wanda and Kelly trotted upstairs and began checking the rooms there. All were devoid of personal items except Abbie's bedroom.

"The bastard has ditched Abbie, but that doesn't make sense."

"If he is on the run, he might consider her a liability," was Kelly's suggestion.

"I considered that, but I don't see him giving up on his plans for her inheritance. Then, she has been unpredictable lately, he may expect her to run off."

"He will probably assume the Trust will look after her," Kelly said.

"And then what? He waits a while and comes after her? He won't be able to get Delaney to do his dirty work again."

"Dreadful thought. We will have to try to get her to make a habit of being careful."

"That didn't work for me at fifteen," Wanda recalled. "Kelly, what reason might there be for the housekeepers stuff to be gone as well?"

"He probably gave her notice. If he was moving, interstate as he claimed, he may not need her. He could hire another locally."

"Yes, and if he has also changed his look and identity, he wouldn't want a link back to Carson. Will you be trying to talk to that woman?"

"Naturally," Kelly assured her.

"You know, this is really going to be hard on Abbie."

"Well, she has Annie and Martin on her side. Both those kids are pretty level-headed."

They began to wander down. "What do you think of the idea of letting Annie move around and touch stuff?" Wanda asked.

"Do you think that wise?"

"I don't think she would pick up anything really bad, but she might get an idea of where he was headed, or doing and thinking."

"It won't be evidence..."
"Of course not but it may give us clues."
"Will you be with her?"
Wanda nodded.
"Ok. Try it when Kaspersky finishes with Abbie. I'll have her put her stuff in the boxes the packers left in there. Tell me later if you intuit anything useful."

Abbie emerged and led Kaspersky to her father's office. The door was wide open and only the furniture remained. She checked all the drawers in the desk, opened the cupboard. They, like the open safe, were empty. David, had already looked inside, and compared it to what Wanda remembered.

"He usually kept this room locked," Abbie muttered. "I'm not surprised there is nothing here."

She turned and walked out, heading for her parent's bedroom. She had not gone in there often, but usually she could see the sorts of fancy stuff her mother liked. The bed was stripped, the chairs devoid of fancy cushions, or her mother's clothes, shoes and things. She did a cursory peek in all the drawers, and the empty wardrobe.

"Mum must have gone with him," Abbie said. "She must have, but she had heaps of clothes. Can I check my room now?"

Kaspersky nodded, and Abbie headed for the stairs. Wanda gestured Annie and Martin into the office.

"Annie, why don't you see if you pick up anything."

"Okay," she agreed, mildly uncertain.

Annie decided that it was a test, but she was glad Wanda was with her. "I'll leave the desk until last..."

None of the random surfaces she touched, even after waiting for some moments, gave her any images. She tried the light switches, the window closures, the door handles – there was nothing. She shook her head at Wanda, and approached the desk. She touched the area in front of the chair. "Nothing."

"There was a thick leather desk protector there," Wanda recalled, "Try the drawers."

Annie shook her head, then shoved the chair with her hip. That didn't give her anything so she went and sat in it. Instantly, she went rigid, and gave an involuntary cry. Wanda went and placed gentle hands on her shoulder, and while aware of Annie's sudden nausea, she was receiving the same images that Annie was.

"Hang in there, Annie," Wanda urged. The images were flickering rapidly, almost too fast even for her to grasp. It all seemed to morph into a sense of the 'aura' of the man who had used the chair.

"Get up, Annie," Wanda directed, sending the request verbally and mentally. She then began a low humming, that was soothing to the ear.

Annie sprang up and was taking deep breaths. "That was horrible. I felt trapped in a dark place. Did you get anything from me?"

"Mainly just a sense of the 'aura' of Carson," Wanda admitted, although she wondered if she could replay that period and slow it down. "I will know him if I encounter him again." She didn't want to say that Annie likely would too, and hoped, that if at some future time Carson tried to get Abbie back, she would sense him and have an instant to react.

"I think that's enough," Wanda told Annie, then glanced at Martin to include him when she asked, "How do you think Abbie will handle this?"

"She's better off without him," Martin stated. His own sense of freedom hadn't abated.

Annie answered more slowly. "Her Dad was pretty good to her, until recently. Not like you and your Dad. I know he went off at her a few times, but she did do some stupid things. Still, he shouldn't have just walked out and left her."

"No," Wanda agreed. "How do you think she will cope when he gets picked up again? There will be more charges, serious ones, and it will probably reach the papers."

"The Hells Angels will be right poisonous," Martin predicted. "Maybe if she stays with you for a while, Annie, she will find out what a decent father is like and pretend she chose to disown him. As far as I'm concerned, he was trying to make her like her mum, obedient, decorative and helpless. Totally reliant on him. Seems she isn't yet."

"My place is small compared to this," Annie remarked. "It will be really different for her. And I don't think her friends will be very nice when they find out what her father did or if they realise she is staying with me..."

Wanda inserted a suggestion. "If they aren't told, I wonder how fast they will find out. If they drop her, showing how hollow and selfish they are, they will be red-faced when they find out Abbie is Maude's daughter and the Hartley heiress."

"They don't think much of Maude," Annie said.

Wanda gestured to head back out into the grand hall, and they were there when Abbie trotted down the stairs, holding something small in her hands.

"Annie, come see Tinker." The something in Abbie's hands said, "Meow."

"You've got a cat?" Annie was instantly diverted.

"You don't think your dog will hurt her?"

"Lucky is still a baby herself," Annie said. "I think she will want to play and they will be company for each other when we're at school."

Martin growled. "Do you mean your bastard of a father left it alone up there?"

"She had milk, and Mrs Buttrose left her food next to the box. She left me a short letter."

"Can I see it?" Wanda asked.

"Detective Kelly took it, but she just said she was sorry not to be able to say good-bye. Dad had just given her notice and she had to pack and head off."

"Have you packed all your stuff?" Wanda asked.

"I think so, but the bed is mine, and the sheets. There should have been two sets of sheets, but I guess the other went with Dad."

"Nothing else of yours missing?"

"No, I checked. I keep my iPod and iPad in my school bag and no one else likes my music."

"We'll get your stuff out, and I think then that you young folk won't be needed. Annie, will your Mum or Dad come to pick you up? David and I can help take the boxes."

Abbie looked at Annie. "Are your folks really alright about me suddenly landing on them?"

Annie grinned. "Mum said she always wanted more than one kid, and I've always wanted a brother or sister, so, while you want to stay, it will be fun."

"Gail is going to call me another charity case."

Martin snorted. "She wouldn't know charity if she fell in it."

"And being called that hasn't hurt me. Anyway, you don't have to tell her. Does she ever come around here?"

"No." Abbie didn't say her father had never encouraged friends coming around.

"Well, we can test how clever she is. She always pretends to know everything." Annie grinned faintly and glanced at Wanda as she went on. "If a charity case like me leaves some sort of contamination, she ought to notice right away, hey? Besides term ends in two days."

Abbie looked around as if trying to memorise the house. "What's going to happen to this place?"

"The agent will find another tenant," Wanda said.

"No, I mean, Detective Kelly and the other one seem awfully interested in everything."

"Well, my guess would be that they want to locate your parents and get to the bottom of their despicable behaviour."

Abbie was startled by her bluntness. Yet she appreciated being told straight.

"He is despicable. He went off and left me."

Annie returned Tinker to her before she started crying again. She wondered why Wanda had been so direct.

"Abbie, I want you to remember this – he didn't go away to punish you for the silly things you've done recently. He went because he is trying to save his hide from going to jail. For that, you are extra baggage. He can move around a lot easier alone."

"What about Mum?"

"I think she'll be fine. She's an adult, used to his ways." Wanda hoped she was right, and Victoria Carson didn't become a liability after Carson got back control of all his money.

"Mum said he loved me," Abbie insisted. She saw Martin shaking his head. "What?"

"He loves himself, and you as a means to more money. If I had been some rich man's son, he'd have probably have had us engaged already and be working out how to take my fortune too."

David, who had been keeping the agent occupied, came over. "Annie's Dad is here."

All of a sudden, Abbie couldn't wait to leave.

Late that night, Abbie lay awake. The Jamieson's spare bed didn't feel like her own, and the cosiness of the room was a bit oppressive. She wasn't going to admit it, but she was glad Annie had volunteered to sleep on a camp bed next to her, even though her mother had said, "Only for tonight."

They had been whispering until Annie's Dad had poked his head in and said, "Go to sleep, you two."

Annie was already asleep now, and her dog and Tinker were curled up together on Lucky's bed. When the two creatures had been introduced, it had been hilarious.

The whole atmosphere in the Jamieson house was unlike anything she could remember. They were effectively strangers, but she had felt genuinely welcomed from the moment she had arrived. More so than with her mum's supposed relatives. She had briefly considered what might have happened had she called her other friends. Probably their parents would have called the police, and had her put with complete strangers. Or if her father had taken her, then changed his mind and dumped her who knew where. That had scared her the most as it brought back the horrible hours when she had been abducted.

As she tried to sleep, some memory of a soothing voice, said to her that it didn't happen, that she was safe, loved, cherished, wanted. She fell asleep and dreamed of being young and carefree, with a sister and mother that loved her.

Episode 27

Upside Down

Chapter 1

Annie thought the car parked outside her house was familiar, and was proved right when she saw Wanda and her mother having coffee together in the kitchen. She waved at the visitor and went through to the back garden where Lucky-pup was yipping excitedly.

Abbie ghosted through after her but went to drop her bag in the spare room. She spotted her own bed, set up and already made and felt a glow of delight. She trotted back to the kitchen.

"You brought my bed! Thank you!"

"We said we would," Wanda grinned. "How was school?"

Abbie laughed. "Gail, Helen and Clare are still clueless, and now I have two weeks without their snide remarks. Have you heard anything more about my dad?"

"No." Wanda's grin disappeared. "The police took his car somewhere, since it would have been towed out of the casino carpark anyway."

"Do they think something happened to him?"

"I don't think so. I take it you haven't heard anything."

"No."

"Are you up to meeting Mr Tyrell tonight or tomorrow?"

"Has he got the results?"

"He didn't say. He was trying to reach your dad and when he couldn't he called Kelso."

"Would I have to go into town?"

"No. Tyrell would be okay with coming here."

Abbie looked to Mrs Jamieson who answered, "It's okay with me." She didn't let on that Wanda had already asked.

"I think I would prefer to be here, then."

"Okay. I will let him know. David can pick him up."

Wanda was back to looking like herself, and Abbie decided that her current demeanour was probably her true persona and a contrast to their first meeting.

Annie returned, having dropped her bag somewhere. She was trying to free Abbie's kitten from playing with her hair. Lucky-pup ran to Abbie and reached up for attention.

When neither girl was looking, Wanda and Marilyn Jamieson exchanged smiles.

When the initial commotion died down, Wanda asked, "Where did David get to?"

Annie said, "He and Dad are discussing something out back."

"Well, there was something we needed to tell you. An apology, really. We hoped to be able to stay and start the self-defence lessons, but we won't be able to. We have to head back to the States next week."

"Oh!" Annie said, deflating. "I mean, I knew you'd have to and all, but..."

"We can keep in touch by the internet, since your folks have met us. I was going to say that David and I thought we could give you two girls and Martin a head start before then – if you are interested."

"Yes!" Abbie said immediately. Annie nodded.

"Maybe I will try for a refresher," Hank Jamieson announced, as he and David came in and made the kitchen feel crowded.

"Feel free," Wanda invited. "So, we'll head off and let you know when to expect us back."

When they got back to Kelso's house, he asked, "How did the

Jamiesons take what you told them?"

"Pretty well," Wanda decided. "I gave Marilyn a brief idea of Carson's status, and the potential of him facing further charges. She is incensed that he would just abandon his child like that. Her maternal instinct is in full swing."

"I think she feels so strongly because when she was a lot younger she had to give up a child," David put in. "Hank says his wife is really into having Abbie staying with them. She wanted lots of kids, but can't have anymore. He thinks Abbie is settling in okay. There's been no friction, but then it has only been two days."

"I expect Tyrell might have a lot of say in her final disposition," Kelso mused.

"So the results do say she is definitely Gabrielle Hartley?" Wanda asked. The former policeman nodded.

"I suggested he come here before seeing Abbie. He will brief us then. He will have the report, but he says he can't let us copy it as it is confidential." Kelso eyed Wanda as he said it.

"I will look them over. I should be able to do a comparison by looking." Her tone was bland, but she produced her phone and deliberately placed it on the table nearby – meeting his eyes.

Kelso made no further comment on that, but switched to other matters. "Did you find anything in Maude's letters?"

"I jotted down ideas that occurred to me, but for finding this Clayton guy, they probably won't help. The letters are nearly twenty years old."

"What about you, David?"

"Well, I have been over the coroner's reports, doctor's records, and the varied media coverage for all the Hartleys. On the surface, their deaths were all understandable, sad events. Except, they all died within a decade, and now we are aware that Carson and probably Delaney, are after the Hartley money."

"Give me your ideas, I will have them followed up," Kelso directed.

"I do intend to look deeper at the data," David told him. "You might get the police forensic pathologists to go over them again too."

"I will. I have also had a word with Des Kingley and Gordon Forrest about a possible leak within the police department. Carson had to have been tipped off."

"What about Robbo's stuff?" Wanda asked.

"We should have it later this evening. Robbo made a notarised statement, enabling Thea to act for him. Fred has taken her to the safe deposit place."

David asked, "How fast can you get DNA tests done if there is anything to use in that stuff."

Kelso considered that. "Two weeks. Do we really need it though? We can pin Carson to Mainwright by matching Robbo and Thea's DNA to the sample the police took."

"True, but on the off chance Carson wasn't lying when he claimed their mother was having an affair, you would be covered."

"You are thorough, lad. I will give you that."

Kelso nodded with approval. "And I have some excellent news. After Carson decamped so abruptly, and his recent actions suggest he could be a dangerous man, the police have more chance of a warrant to search the Stillman unit, to see if there is a clue to where he might have gone."

"Okay!" Wanda said with relish. "So if they find anything in there that I saw at his house – we will have that connection."

"He wasn't doing the clearing out," Kelso told her. "The neighbours only saw catering vans – like when he has fancy dinners for clients. Likely they were the cleaners an all the personal stuff went off with them."

"When Abbie saw her father during the night – Thursday – he might have been sneaking stuff out then," David suggested. "Can that be followed up?"

Kelso nodded. "Yes, and the accounts from young Martin

and Abbie link the fake nurse to the taxi fare and to Carson. They did find prints on the gloves you found, David. Inside and out."

Wanda grinned faintly. "An amateur! So that nails Carson for trying to get the better of me."

"Yes, but linking him to earlier crimes, may not be easy," Kelso reminded them.

"You can still call us to pick our brains," Wanda invited.

"Says the vengeful bitch I married," David warned.

Chapter 2

"So I am really Gabrielle Hartley?" Abbie asked, even though Tyrell had already said so. "So what does that mean?"

Abbie's hand continued to pat the kitten on her lap. Tinker was perfectly at peace, a complete contrast to how she felt. She wished there was someone to give her advice, and thoughts of her parents only made her seem more of a child. Annie and her parents had tactfully retreated, leaving her and Tyrell together. Even Wanda had slipped out.

Tyrell hid a sigh, wondering what the girl was afraid of. "As I explained. You are a member of the Hartley family, and there is a trust fund that is now yours. It will provide you with an income and once you are an adult, you will be free to do what you wish."

"I got that part," Abbie said. "I heard that this trust is a lot of money. Can I just leave school? Do what I please? Buy whatever I want?"

It wasn't exactly what she was trying to express, but how do you say, "Can I tell my parents to get lost and stay that way?"

"Do you want to leave school?" Tyrell asked gently. He glanced up as Wanda brought a tray into the room.

"Chocolate," Wanda said to Abbie.

"Coffee," she said giving a cup to Tyrell.

"Why don't you stay?" he invited. "I feel there is a generation gap happening here. You are nearer to Gabrielle's age."

Wanda noticed Abbie flinch at being addressed that way. She said, "If you want me to interpret age 15, you don't know who you're asking. At that age, I couldn't get away from my father, or school, fast enough."

"Why?" Abbie asked, glad of a distraction.

"Because my teachers couldn't teach me what I wanted to know, and my father wouldn't let me do what I wanted to do."

154

"What was that?" Abbie was hooked. In some ways Wanda had been like her.

"To become filthy rich before I turned 23," Wanda said truthfully.

"Seems like I am already rich," Abbie said.

"And your father saved you the trouble of ditching him," Wanda pointed out. "And since he is not here to tell you what to think, what do you want to do with your life? Quit school? Get married? Go on the dole?"

"What did you do at 15?"

"Quit school, for one," Wanda admitted. "Lived with a bloke for a while. Lived on the streets for a while until I got sick and picked up."

Abbie shuddered at the ideas Wanda's words evoked. "How did you survive?"

"Stole stuff. Stole money."

"Didn't you get caught?"

"Yes. I spent a year in a training centre. It wasn't a picnic."

"I don't know what I want to do," Abbie admitted. "I like designing clothes, but I don't know how that would make money for me."

"You're good at maths. Did you ever consider where that could take you?"

"Dad said –"

"Forget what he said," Wanda said sharply.

"Well, no, then."

"Okay. That is one advantage of school – opens you up to opportunities. Does your school have a careers counsellor or some such?"

"Yes, why?"

"They ought to have access to all sorts of graduate and post graduate courses and what might suit you and what you'd need to get into them. They will probably give you better ideas than I ever got."

"What did they tell you?"

"Well, since I kept ditching classes, they figured I wasn't fit for anything needing a brain. So....do you want to stay at school?"

Abbie nodded. It sounded better that some alternatives.

Tyrell nodded as Wanda explained, "You will still be able to do that."

"But where will I have to live?" Abbie blurted.

Wanda glanced at Tyrell, who took the hint. "Would you be happy to stay here?"

"I don't really belong here. I mean, I'd be an extra mouth to feed. Gail says Annie's parents aren't rich like mine."

Wanda made a rude noise. "Your friend Gail is your age. How much of family finances do you understand?"

"Well, Daddy would get me whatever I wanted. Annie says she has to save up for the things she wants."

"Does your friend Gail get spoilt rotten by her father?"

Abbie blinked. She didn't know. But Gail had pinched her iPad for ages.

"There's a difference between 'want' and 'need'," Wanda told Abbie. People can have all they need and be perfectly happy without having a lot of expensive stuff. It makes the extras worth much more when you have to wait for them."

"Mr and Mrs Jamison are quite happy for you to stay here," Tyrell assured Abbie. "However, if you would prefer to live somewhere else, that could be arranged."

"Where?"

"We would find a suitable foster family," Tyrell suggested.

"No. It's okay. I like Annie. But when Gail finds out, she will call me a charity case too."

"What say we leave your know it all friend out of this," Wanda suggested. "We are considering you what you want, and giving you a say in it."

"Here isn't like home," Abbie said. "There's less space, and Annie's parents aren't at all like mine. They will expect me to be like Annie, but I've never had to do the stuff she does."

"Ah, that." Wanda pretended it was a problem, then said, "Wouldn't you want to have your own apartment one day?"

"Daddy said I'd stay with them until I was married."

"Daddy said!" Wanda muttered. "Didn't I say to leave him out of this? I think he was trying to turn you into a helpless, dependent parasite."

That caused Abbie to twist, as if about to retort. When she didn't, Wanda asked, "What?"

"My mum is like that. Dad tells her what to do, how to act – all that. Annie said she would teach me to cook."

"And her mum would be delighted to teach you things too. You just need to be willing to try and prepared to ask."

"Yeah, alright. I think I'd like to be able to be independent."

Tyrell took the opportunity to explain, "The Hartley Trust would pay for all your schooling costs and any other major expenses. You could pay the Jamiesons a small amount each week for board, or rather we would."

"And Mrs Jamieson could help you budget with the allowance you get," Wanda added slyly.

"If my dad comes back, will I have to go back and live with him?"

"No." Tyrell's answer was emphatic. "I am liaising with the Department of Health and Human Services. We will endorse your decision to stay with the Jamiesons. In other circumstances, you would have been put in with a foster family anyway."

"But Dad..."

"He left you on your own," Wanda reminded her.

"But isn't he my legal guardian?"

"He's lost that privilege as far as I am concerned. Besides... Tyrell, did you tell her all the DNA results?"

"Ah, no," Tyrell admitted. He seemed to flush faintly. "I will let you, if you wish."

"What are you talking about?" Abbie asked.

"Tyrell told you that Maude Hartley had twins, didn't he?"

"Yes."

"Well, at about the time you and the other girl were conceived, Maude had sex with two different men. Her twins, were actually fathered by two different men."

Abbie looked stunned, but then something occurred to her. "At school, when they taught us about that stuff, they said once a woman is pregnant, she's ..."

"Yeah, that's usual," Wanda agreed. "But this is a rare event. What it means, in your case, is Jeremy Carson is not your biological dad."

It was like the sun had begun to shine directly into the room. Abbie sat up straighter and began to smile. Finally she asked, "So, I won't have to go and live with Maude?"

Tyrell shook his head. "She is, however, looking forward to seeing you."

"What if she doesn't like me?"

Chapter 3

The dinner area at the Community House was decorated for a party.

"What's going on?" Abbie asked, seeing the balloons and streamers. "Is someone here having a birthday?"

"I think this is for you," Annie said, grinning. "Oh, Wanda has come with Mr Tyrell. Wanda gets on great with Maude."

"What will I say to her?"

"Who? Maude? Tell her you only just found out about her," Annie suggested. "I bet she'll have so many questions for you. And Wanda says she can do complicated sums in her head. But she can't put the working out on paper."

"Really, how did you find out about that?"

"Wanda did."

"How come Maude is here with all the old people?"

"The people here look after her, and she is good with the poor mind wandering ones."

Tyrell went in through some doors and Wanda came over. "Just be yourself, Abbie. Don't talk too fast, and if you ask Maude a question, let her answer it in her own time. Don't be surprised if she gets emotional. It has been a long time since she last saw you."

Abbie nodded, seeing Tyrell returning with a short woman, obviously dressed up for the occasion, with permed hair, a pearl necklace, and clutching a picture frame.

"Gabrielle, this is Maude. Your mother."

"Gabbie, you're big!" Maude greeted, her eyes full of moisture. "You really alive."

She seemed afraid to come too close, but something in Abbie responded. Those who had raised her had always been reserved, almost distant, were rarely demonstrative.

"I guess I must be, alive I mean." She moved to give Maude a hug. "Though I'm used to being called Abbie."

"Gabbie? Abbie? Like Abbie," Maude announced. Then she turned the photo frame so Abbie could see it. "You small last time. That you, next to Ellie."

Abbie was hardly aware of the group being ushered through to the dining area, and a group of chairs and couches. "It's odd to think I have a twin."

"Had. My Ellie dead."

"And I thought you were dead, since my dad looked after me."

Maude twisted around. "Where's Wally? He here too?"

"No, Maude, Abbie's father couldn't be here today," Wanda told her.

"Good. Wally think me stupid. Act now like I not here."

Abbie decided this woman, her real mother, had her dad well figured out. "My dad's name is Jeremy."

"Was Wally," Maude insisted.

"Mr Tyrell said he actually isn't my real father," Abbie said and was surprised when Maude chuckled.

"Wally not so smart, but he look after you okay."

Maude pulled Abbie down beside her onto one of the couches. "You really Clay's girl. Clay nicer than Wally."

The observers in the group, Annie, Tyrell and Wanda, sat back, smiling. Abbie needed have worried. Maude had taken to her at once and had plenty of questions. When the emotional dam finally burst, Abbie felt it natural to give the woman, who didn't sound mad, or simple, a hug. It was an odd feeling though, like she was the mother, not the daughter.

One of the house staff approached, an announced the party food was ready. Abbie, hid the thought that it looked like a kid's party, because Maude rubbed her eyes and said, "Asked for all favourite things."

As if she sensed an awkward moment, Wanda said, "You know, Maude, you have given me a whole lot of new ideas for the next kid's party I do. Fancy, colour sprinkles on bread and butter. And what are these?"

"Crackles. Got bubbles in chocolate."

It jolted Abbie into realising, Maude was remembering a time over a decade before, and some deep memory stirred.

"Purple cupcakes," she said aloud.

"Yes. Yes. Ellie like pink. What you drink?"

"What do you have?"

"Rainbow drinks. Red, green, yellow, orange."

More memories stirred. "Green. I haven't had that since I was really little." Abbie remembered Victoria giving her some occasionally. Probably when her father wasn't around. When she had got a bit older, her birthday parties were held at places with structured activities and catered food."

"Annie, what you drink?"

"I'll have orange," Annie decided.

"Ellie like orange. It like she here too."

Abbie murmured in Annie's ear. "Not sure if I like that idea."

Annie, equally quietly said, "For today. I'll pretend. I don't want to spoil her day."

When Wanda sensed Abbie was becoming overwhelmed, she inserted questions to Maude that changed the topic and got Maude and Tyrell taking about Maude's family. Tyrell added his recollections of Maude's brothers, and inserted the detail that "Clay" had been a friend to both of them.

Two hours passed very quickly, but Maude looked to be tiring. Wanda decided on a distraction.

"What you got?" Maude asked as she opened up a small laptop computer.

"I promised you a glimpse of my two little monkeys," Wanda said. "I had my sister do a short video of them in action."

Abbie and Abbie were interested as well. Maude was soon chuckling. "Gabbie and Ellie behave better."

"Yeah, well, my father calls it karma."

"How come," Annie asked. "Because you were a brat?"

"Something like that," Wanda agreed.

"Is that your sister?" Abbie asked.

"Yes. Elisabeth. She often stays with Dad when her new husband is busy."

"He's a hunk," Maude announced when Derek came into the frame and scooped up both kids. Davy waved, and Katy was sending sloppy kisses.

"You go home soon," Maude stated.

"Yes, we have to go home next week," Wanda told her, and then found herself being hugged by Maude.

"They lucky kids. You go. You found my Gabbie."

"Reckon you can look at a screen like that and talk to me through it?"

"How do that?"

"Another time, we'll try it," Wanda promised. "But we need to head off now."

"No. No. Wait." Maude began checking her pockets, but Tyrell handed her a box. "This for Gabbie...Abbie." Maude emphasised the name as she handed the box over.

Surprised, Abbie opened it. "Oh! It's lovely." It was a delicate gold chain with little ornaments dangling from it.

Maude pointed to them. "Each for birthday missed."

Abbie hugged Maude again. "I don't have anything for you."

"I have you back. You visit with Annie and scout girls?"

Abbie nodded.

"And don't let Wally have that."

"No way," Abbie promised.

"Abbie is staying with Annie now," Wanda said casually.

"Good. Don't want Wally make her hate me."

"He won't," Abbie promised, glad that she didn't ask why she wasn't with 'Wally'.

Wanda returned to Kelso's after seeing the two girls home. The ever obliging Fred had been their driver. She was pleased with the outcome, which she reported to David and Kelso, and happy to return to some of the computer searching she was doing.

"They've got the warrant to search the Stillman unit," Kelso announced, getting the immediate attention of his two American friends. "Des wants both of you on the team that goes in. You will be working with the detectives at Bellfield."

"When?" David sprang up from the computer search he was doing.

"As soon as you can get there."

"Right!" Wanda announced, up and moving in the same instant. "I want to get a few things from our room."

For a moment, David seemed to be waiting for her, but suddenly followed her.

When they both emerged, they had changed into the all black protective gear they had worn for the raid in the park.

"Do you expect trouble?" Kelso asked, for Wanda had also done a quick job of changing her face.

"Not specially. I'm keeping low profile." In fact, she had felt the need to be prepared for the unexpected. If Stillman was Carson as they believed, he had proved to have a dangerous side. He had tried to silence her for what she could tell about him and if Stillman was his fall-back ID, he would not want the stuff he had in there looked at. It was the act of heeding such hunches that had saved her and others on more than a few occasions. She had in her pockets a set of master keys, several highly confidential electronic devices, a digital camera and a signal jammer.

Two police cars had bracketed the unit's roll up door, and the night duty manager had the master key, but he was twisting and looking everywhere, as if afraid of being seen there. Wanda and David had parked along the main road and approached on foot.

Once they arrived, Kaspersky directed the manager to open the unit. He did as told, not having a choice, but he stood aside quickly and let the police open the roll up door. He watched the two policemen, and studied the two later arrivals.

Wanda stopped at the door and let David take a high definition video of what they saw. It seemed like a head high wall of stacked boxes – all an anonymous beige, unmarked and identical in size. Kelly and Kaspersky had gone to each end of the wall, and begun lifting boxes down. They opened several and found shredded paper.

"Camouflage," David decided. "So casual observers see nothing."

Wanda had other ideas, and the nerves in her spine were tingling – her danger sense was rousing. She felt in her pocket and activated the signal jammer. She began moving boxes from the middle of the wall so that David could film behind them. The two detectives had reached the boxes at the back, which were heavier, and were starting to look within. David moved between them, recording, while Wanda used instinct to select seemingly random boxes, which she took back near the entrance. She was back behind the box wall, when she suddenly straightened and looked around. Her danger sense had ramped up, like someone had just tapped her on the back. She moved to one of the boxes still part of the wall, and said, "Dav! Check this."

David dropped the camera so it hung from a strap around his neck, and took one of the electronic devices Wanda handed him. She had another. They both ran the devices over the outer side of the boxes.

David's device beeped. He called out a warning, "Some boxes contain explosives or chemicals."

"Out!" Kaspersky ordered. He and Kelly dropped what they were looking at immediately.

Wanda and David moved at the same time, but Wanda stopped near the door to grab two boxes. A box right at the back burst into explosive flame, setting off several others. The heat blasted out through the door. David grabbed the box from Wanda, and expected her to follow, but she grabbed another.

David dropped his box, and patted his hair feeling sparks land. Wanda came out, partly wet, for the sprinklers inside had come on, but only had an effect near the door. Further in, the water instantly became steam.

Outside, Kaspersky was calling the fire brigade, and Kelly moved to check on the two civilian consultants.

"You look a bit singed," he noted. "You should have left those boxes."

"They may have useful contents," Wanda said, ignoring the mild reprimand. "They didn't feel like a lot of the other boxes."

Kelly didn't push it. He was angry, because the explosions were obviously intended to destroy evidence, and likely to cause harm to the searchers. He moved away to where the night duty manager was trying to talk to Kaspersky, insisting he tell the fire trucks to hurry, that the flames might get to the adjoining units.

David suddenly wrenched the camera from around his neck and shoved it at his wife. Without explanation, he slipped into the crowd that hadn't taken long to start forming. Wanda took it and one of the boxes she'd rescued to the police car. She went back for the other, which was under Kaspersky's eye, and it joined the other. She leant against the police car and took the signal jammer from her pocket. The explosions had to have been detonated remotely, but the device should have scrambled the signal. Unless the signal was from really close by. She began to scan the faces of the crowd. She doubted that Carson would be here, but the night manager might have warned someone of the raid. Someone who lived fairly close. Her mind added up the time from when Kelso had been called. It had taken her and David about twenty minutes to get there. Her eyes went back to the night manager. He was twitchy, unable to keep still. He was staring at the flames threatening the units on each side. She carefully reached out to sense his mind. Guilt and anxiety were the dominant emotions. Wanda edged back to where Kelly was keeping the onlookers back. Two onlookers were staring at the flames – she guessed they might be the unit holders. Most of the others fixated on the flames were looking at the main fire. She watched one man carefully easing himself to the front of the crowd, then just as subtly allowing the crowd to push him back. When he was out of the crowd, Wanda edged away from the police car and began to follow him, keeping to the shadows.

As he walked, the man took out his phone and made a call. Wanda closed the distance to listen.

"J, it's Lonny. Everything inside is char." He listened, "No, they must have got out. Don't look like anyone's hurt." He listened some more. The fire truck sirens were getting very loud. "What? 2 cars, four cops."

He ended the call, oblivious to the shadow that followed him until he entered a building, memorised the address, and then returned to the scene of the activity.

When Wanda returned, she saw David had a dark clad man, handcuffed and cursing, being pushed down into Kelly's car. The fire truck had arrived and were already projecting high pressure hoses onto the roof of the two adjoining units and into the still fiercely burning one.

The four detectives stationed at Bellfield, studied the video David was projecting onto a white wall. When asked, he enlarged sections of the film to show the older, further in boxes. The camera had still been running when Kaspersky had ordered them out, so the actual first explosion was heard but not seen directly – just as the ambient flare of orange light. The video ended soon after.

Tony Mendes, now back on duty, asked, "How does what we saw here compare to the glimpse you had the other week?"

Kaspersky answered that. "The wall of identical boxes is new." He turned to David. "The box with the incendiary, where was that?"

"It was one of the box wall."

"That fire was laid deliberately," Mendes decided. "It explains the boxes of shredded paper. I expect the arson guys will find most of those boxes contained flammable stuff."

"There were four or five separate explosions," Wanda told him. "Whoever planted them wanted to ensure everything was destroyed."

"You and David suddenly started checking boxes with those devices of yours. What made you suspect trouble?"

"I was already twitchy because of the set-up," Wanda admitted. The local men nodded, understanding that feeling. "I think I started to smell something chemical." That answer satisfied them, but the true reason, even Kelly might have found hard to believe.

"Those boxes you brought out, what made you pick them? Were there markings on them?" Mendes went on.

"As things turned out, I hope they were lucky dips. They weren't light, but they felt different to most of the others. Less densely solid perhaps, or the others were stacked paper files and these weren't."

Wanda saw the detective nodding again. He asked her, "Do you want to see what you got?"

Knowing the other four men were equally curious, she merely remarked, "I thought you'd never ask. Have they been tested for prints?"

Mendes pulled on gloves before finding a sharp knife to slip open the packing tape. The box was also a generic packing box, but of a different type to those in the outer wall.

"David, if you would, can you record what's inside?"

Without answering, David disconnected the digital recorder from the projector, made sure the new video would be in a separate file, and nodded when he was ready.

From the first box, Mendes took a locked deed box, a box of the old six-inch floppy discs, and a few of the less old three inch ones. He looked at some of the discs and showed the labels to the camera. The locked deed box would have been put aside, but Wanda produced her key set and the second key she tried, opened it. Inside was a small box with some early usb drives, a roll of printouts, and several small journal books and brochures. Each was described for the video and tagged for evidence,

The second box caused Wanda to murmur 'Bingo'. Mendes took from it a smaller box, that she had seen at Carson's house, labelled 'Family'. She noted that fact formally, to Mendes. Under that, had been another locked deed box, which when opened, proved to be the jackpot. Bundles of passport wallets and paper documents in more than one name. As Mendes read them out, Wanda felt a growing sense of excitement.

"I think we need to get the Chief Super in on this," Mendes remarked.

"It will need to be kept under wraps if we want a chance to get Carson. Some of these names were plastered over the newspapers years back." That comment came from the senior detective at Bellfield, Hank Caruthers. He had been on the force for nearly forty years and had an excellent memory.

David added, "And it confirms Robbo Mainwright's contention that Carson is the man he knew of as his father."

"Don't go and tell him yet," Caruthers advised.

David nodded. They would find out when their DNA result came through, unless their mother had played around, but he had found no hint that was likely. Dolly Mainwright had an impeccable reputation.

The following day, Des Kingley invited Wanda and David to his office.

"You did good work. I don't know how you happened to pick those boxes, but we have now linked Stillman to some wanted criminals of the past."

"And to Carson," Wanda reminded him. "Would we be allowed access to the information we found?"

"Well, we have our tech experts working to access the information. They have to find a way to play the discs. You'll be leaving soon, won't you?"

"We will be, yes," Wanda admitted. "However, we told Kelso that we wanted to keep investigating some older events."

"Such as?" Kingley asked.

"The Carson/Delaney connection and their association with Maude Hartley."

"What makes you think the information you found will help?"

"I had a quick look at the printouts and notebooks in one of the deed boxes," Wanda explained. "I think they are related to some hand written notes we found when the scout house was being cleared out. It is possible one or more of the discs are copies of one we found there."

"That is interesting. What else can you tell me?"

"The house the scouts were given, was once owned by Charles Hartley, Maude's brother," David added. "The notes appeared to be a horse race winner prediction algorithm. One of the names on the IDs that were found in the unit was Jacob Hillier. He was involved in a race prediction operation."

"We probably can't prosecute him for that," Kingley considered. "How will it help you?"

"We aren't sure yet. David and I feel that it was odd how Charles Hartley died and something like his algorithm was used to swindle money from hopeful punters."

"Yes, Kelso mentioned your theory. I have no problem with you continuing to look into that angle. I doubt that you can do much to proove the connection."

"I realise that, Sir, but I am not ready to give up yet," David told him.

"If we get anywhere with the discs, I will be in touch," Kingley promised.

"If your tech guys have trouble, I have some tech geek friends who may be able to help," David offered.

"I will keep that in mind," Kingley said, then changed subjects. "Now, I have seen your request for bone fragments from the scout house skeletons. What is your interest there?"

"Just being thorough," David told him. "Between us, Wanda and I, we have encountered some devious attempts to fake identification evidence."

"DNA was used to identify, or try to identify those poor children. Twelve or so years ago, that wasn't a well-known technique. It is not likely they predicted it."

"True, Sir," Wanda agreed. "But the report stated that they had found hair in the child's clothing and used that to do the test. In the States, I can get a DNA test done on the bones. I would really like to be sure whether or not the little girl was Ellie Hartley. We might as well check the other skeleton as well."

"Very well, I well arrange authorisation for that request. I assume you will still be investigating Carson when you have gone home?" He was watching Wanda for a reaction, but she gave none.

"There's only so much we can do from over there. Mainly computer searches. I have access to a highly skilled computer expert. If you need help tracing a money trail between countries, we might be able to help."

"And tracing phone calls," David added.

"I will see what our Australian Police can do, first," Kingley said with a faint smile. "You have stirred up a lot of leads to old cases and to current ones. I will keep your offer in mind. However, I think you should both spend a few days as tourists before you go home.”

“Oh, we will be,” Wanda admitted. “The Jamiesons, the people who took in Abbie Carson, have invited us to some wildlife sanctuary.”

“Which might be so they can have a day off the lessons we are giving the girls and their friend Martin,” David added with a grin.

“Self-defence, I believe,” Kingley said, surprising them that he knew. “It’s an excellent idea. Do you think Carson might intend trying to get his daughter back in the future?”

Wanda nodded, expression serious.

“I can’t believe that I never once suspected Carson capable of what he has done recently. It seems your presence has been the catalyst to break down his façade.”

Kingley stared past both of his guests for a while, then said, “I think I will ask Gordon Forrest to arrange access for you so you can look in official files. I feel certain you won’t misuse the privilege. There may be some documents related to secrecy that will need to be signed.”

“That would be expected,” David agreed.

“You will be keeping in touch with my former superior?”

“Of course. And I hope he will be able to keep us abreast of selected investigations. He is to give us notice of when Carson is due in court.”

“Will you be returning if you are needed for that?”

“Unless we are tied up elsewhere,” Wanda gave the proviso. “Otherwise, I wouldn’t miss it.”

“If he is sentenced and incarcerated for the two recent serious things,” David commented. “We will still continue looking into his past. There are aspects of the business with Abbie that unsettle us.”

“You can go for it on those old cases, provided you keep Kelso updated. So go and be tourists and have a safe trip back home.”

"It's a pity I didn't know about the house sooner," Abbie remarked. "It's hard to believe I used to live here."

"It was a dump for years. If you had seen it earlier, you probably wouldn't have recognised anything, even if you had been old enough to remember," Martin told her.

The block where Maude's old home had been was now completely cleared of everything, rubble and plants. It was ready for the new structure, designed by Hank Jamieson, to be built.

"Naomi's dad took photos and videos of the place when they were given it, and at each stage. You might be able to look at that," Annie suggested.

Abbie didn't answer, because Naomi and Karen in their scout uniforms were coming to join them. The scouts had just held a dedication and ground-breaking ceremony, with the local paper recording the event. Maude Hartley, the guest of honour, stood next to Tyrell, dressed as she had been for her first meeting with the grown Abbie.

"Come on over," Naomi invited. "We are having morning tea for the guests and interested observers."

Karen added, "The building, when it is finished is to be called the Charles Hartley Scout Hall."

"I thought you were going to name it after Maude," Annie commented.

"Maude requested the change, and none of us objected. Oh, and the paper guy got a great photo of your dog digging beside Mr Baxter."

"I suppose I had better go and get her," Annie decided. "She didn't want to move out of the way, so I left her with Dad."

"I saw the plans your dad did," Karen enthused. "They are amazing! It's going to be two levels, but without being too much higher than the nearby houses.”

“I saw dad’s sketches,” Annie told her. “It would have been good if Wanda and David could have been here today. They helped Maude so much.” She glanced that way, and saw Maude was now cuddling Lucky-pup.

“They are probably halfway across the ocean by now,” Martin mused, for the American couple had flown out from Tullamarine early that day. “Would we be able to get a copy of today’s video to send them?”

“I’ll ask Mr Lowry,” Naomi promised. “He’s the guy doing the recording. We can send them photos of the progress too.”

“Dad really enjoyed planning the building,” Annie said, as they began walking back to the block. “I heard him tell mum he might start his own agency specialising in rebuilds for people. He says a lot of people are buying old houses and pulling them down so they can build a new place.”

“Would that mean you won’t need to move schools again next year?” Naomi asked.

“It would be good if I can stay. I like it here.”

“Yeah, so much happens around here,” Martin said with a faint grin. “I wonder if your second term at Bellfield will be less interesting.”

“What are you getting at, Kemple?” Karen demanded.

Martin waved at the vacant block. “All this...” Only Annie and Abbie knew he meant more than that. “I mean, Annie was only here a week and she was known to the police.” Martin grinned.

“Thanks to you!” Annie retorted. “At least you’ve been civilised now!”

The other three girls exchanged knowing glances.

Later that day, Abbie sat on Annie’s bed watching a show on Netflix using her computer.

“You haven’t told Naomi about me, have you?”

“It’s not my secret to tell,” Annie told her.

"Do you think I should tell people?"

"What's Mr Tyrell think?" Annie asked instead.

"I think he is humouring me."

"Or letting you get used to your new name and stuff."

"I don't feel any different – except confused. I got used to what Daddy expected, and Mr Tyrell seems to expect something else."

Annie thought on that. "He's old. I guess he keeps thinking of the Hartley's from way back."

"It's going to come out sooner or later," Abbie guessed. "I just don't want Gail, Clare and Helen to know yet."

"The school with have to know, I suppose," Annie said. "Since only your dad knows if he intends to keep paying your school fees."

"And I am staying here now, so I suppose your folks will have to be my home contacts, or Mr Tyrell will," Abbie considered. "Maybe I will let out that I am staying with you. While my parents are away – overseas or something. See how they react."

"Think she will lose interest in you?" Annie asked.

Abbie shrugged. "I do feel like a traitor, keeping secrets from them, but I am tired of Gail bossing me around, and expecting me to take a turn buying lunches. They aren't happy when I keep saying I can't."

"You shouldn't have to," Annie said. "Or they should accept that you can't."

"And if she gets any bitchier, and starts calling me a charity case, I'll tell her where to go."

"Do you know why that doesn't bother me?" Annie asked.

"No."

"Because I know better. And, I consider her trying to put me down as a sign that's she's jealous of me."

"How do you figure that?"

"She probably won't agree, but that's how Dad told me to think about it."

"I really like your Dad and Mum," Abbie affirmed. "And I like Karen and Naomi too. I never gave myself a chance to know them. All the others in the class are probably nice too, even Martin. I did like him until Daddy told him to stay away. Then he started looking like a tramp and they started saying he was into drugs and all."

"I like Martin too, and I am glad all that has been sorted. The police are on his side now too."

"So, I might tell Naomi and Karen about me too."

"What about Mrs Sutton?"

"Maybe. I will let Mr Gill find out from someone else. He probably won't believe me if I did. Anyway, I think I would like to be called Abbie Carson still, for a while."

"Less confusing," Annie considered. "But what if your dad gets found and the newspapers found out what he's done?"

"Then I tell people he wasn't ever really my dad," Abbie decided. "And he's not, as you know. So I can say I have been taken in by the Hartley Foundation as a-"

"Charity case?" Annie giggled.

"I can't get away from that can I?"

"Nope!"

Marilyn Jamieson poked her head in the door. "Good show?" she asked.

"It's okay," Annie told her. "Do you want something, Mum?"

"Actually, I came to give you something. I've had it tucked away for years, keeping it safe as we moved around."

Annie took a little box from her mother and opened it. She had not even seen the box before.

"Hey! It's a bracelet, like yours, Abbie." She lifted it out and examined the dangling ornaments. There were only four. "Thanks, Mum. I'll keep it safe."

"You can add more ornaments to it. There are hundreds of them, or so I'm told."

"I will check it out on the internet," Annie decided aloud.

"Abbie? Can I see yours? To see if any are the same?"

Abbie jumped up, upsetting Tinker and causing Lucky-pup to start jumping around. "I'll get the necklace too."

"Might make us like twins," Annie joked. As she said it, she felt a shiver.

"Maybe it does," Marilyn smiled and left.

"Here," Abbie announced, plopping back onto the bed. "That one looks exactly like mine. It might have come from the same shop. I can't remember when Mum gave me mine – it was already too small for me. These are for little kids, and might have been bought for twins."

"I said something like that to mum," Annie admitted. "But I'm not going to say that to anyone else. These things were probably the rage when we were little. Anyway, the actual ornaments are different."

"Mine must have come from Maude in the first place. How else would she think to get me the necklace?"

"That's a point." Annie was checking the necklace to see if any of those ornaments were the same as the four on her bracelet, or those on Abbie's. All were different.

"Do you think it is fluke, or Maude remembered what I had?"

"Maude does have a good memory, Wanda said. Or they might put out new ones every so often," Annie said.

Epilogue

(Annie POV)

Long after Mum insisted we stop talking and go to bed, I found myself, still awake. I was thinking of all the things that had happened since I had arrived in Bellfield. It reminded me that I hadn't written in my journal for a while. I could add more about the outcomes of my odd visions – a lot of things. So I twisted and took the journal and a pen from the drawer beside my bed, and unhooked my little torch from the hook on the side of the drawers. It wouldn't be the first time I'd made a tent of my bedding so I could read or write.

Two pages later, I felt I had covered everything. But there was one thing I wondered if I should add. The odd shiver I had felt when I had mentioned 'twins'. Maybe it was because Abbie had once been a twin. It hadn't been as intense as some of the flashes I'd had, but I had seen a brief glimpse of two bracelets hanging from two hands, together.

Perhaps by some fluke, mine had been Ellie Hartley's, and Delaney had found it and sold it. She could imagine Delaney doing that. But Ellie Hartley was definitely dead, and her parents weren't related to Abbie's. It had to be a coincidence. It was possible her parents had bought it. They had lived in Melbourne for a bit when she was little, or so they'd told her.

I was yawning now, so I put everything away. As I got into a comfortable position to sleep, I recalled the past few days. Mum and Dad had taken time off to take me and Abbie to various places neither of us had ever been. The first couple of times, we'd had Wanda and David join us. I wondered how their kids would like the stuffed koala and kangaroo toys bought at the sanctuary. They would be a novelty to US kids.

That made me recall the self-defence lessons, and seeing Wanda toss my dad. I should keep practicing so I could be that good. It will be fun when we do the lessons in PE. Abbie had been like one possessed, determined to learn fast. I could guess why. She would be better at it than Gail, Helen and Clare – if they deigned to try it.

Yes, second term was going to be interesting too.

Look out for Season Two of Touching Other Lives.

Also by Margaret Gregory
<u>TYMOREAN TRUST SERIES</u>: (Fantasy)
Book 1 - Power Rising
Book 2 - Great Ones
Book 3 - The Return to Earth
Book 4 – Earth Mission
Book 5 – Alien Contact
Book 6 - Invasion
<u>ATAPI SORCERESS SERIES</u>: (Fantasy)
Prequel – Korvu: The Beginning
Book 1- The Wild One
Book 2 – Atapi Sorceress
<u>THE THIRD GENERATION SERIES</u>:(Fantasy)
Book 1 - Wanda: From Bad to Worse
Book 2 - Wanda: Choosing Crime
Wanda – Early Days (anthology) Book 1 and 2
Book 3 – Wanda: Risking Life to Live
Book 4 – Erin: The Forcing of Wisdom
Book 5 – Wanda: A New Life Part 1 – Hidden Secrets
Book 6 – Wanda: A New Life Part 2 – First Mission
Book 7 – Wanda: Full Circle
The Serpent's Shadow
Royal Favour
Foreign Agent - Thief
Prisoner - Spy

<u>HOLDER OF SECRETS SERIES</u>:
Unregarded
Unsuspected
Unrepentant

<u>STAND ALONE</u>
The Magpie's Daughter
The Chance to be Me
Maeven: Dragon Thief